AF429518

Buckman Publishing LLC
est. 2018
1448 NE 28th Ave
Portland, Oregon 97232
buckmanjournal.com

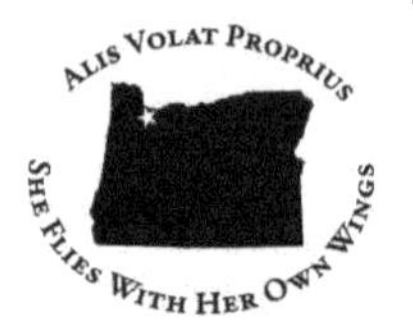

Congratulations! A Buckman production is in your hands! We're an unorthodox operation that continues the daredevil tradition of literature, printing new sparks that ignite imagination. Proudly independent, Buckman's defiant attitude aims to inspire and increase readership in greater society.

Words © 2024 Frances Badalamenti
Cover & Photography © 2024
Aaron Wessling
Book Design: Ellen Robinette
Typefaces: Garamond Premier Pro,
SARABUN, **INTER TIGHT**

ISBN:
9798990017436
LCCN:
2024944243

This is a work of fiction. Names, characters, places, and incidents either are the products of the author's imagination or are used fictitiously. Any resemblance to actual persons, living or dead, businesses, companies, events, or locales is entirely coincidental.

Buckman operates from our home in the upper left of Turtle Island at the confluence of the Whilamut and Wimahl rivers, among the waters and lands of the Cayuse, Clackamas, Multnomah, St'pulmsh (Cowlitz) Umatilla, Walla Walla, and Watlala peoples.

READ THIS BOOK WHEREVER BOOKS CAN BE READ

MANY SEASONS

A novel by Frances Badalamenti

With photography by Aaron Wessling

For all the mothers.

CONTENTS

PROLOGUE

There's a shrub outside the bedroom window that comes alive with these bright, golden-hued flowers in springtime. I've never seen this kind of flowering shrub before. It's an unkempt and beautiful plant.

As the season unfolds and the sun begins to warm, the buds go to bloom and the branches of the shrub inch closer and closer until they reach the window.

Maybe it took a few springs for them to get there. It may have been that first spring, but at the time, my mind was so muddled with love and weed that I don't quite remember. I do remember that once, the branches actually came through the window when it was left open. The flowers were reaching out to us.

That was when we were falling in love: a painful, confusing kind of love.

I wake up in Drew's bed and stare at the blossoming shrub. The sun is warm and bright and the wooden window frame is cracked open a few inches. I feel a subtle cool breeze on my skin. The earthy scents and the sprouting of an Oregon spring are still a novelty. I only know autumn, then winter. Winter was so long and dark and sad—so the sun this morning feels immensely hopeful, kind.

I look at this person next to me. He's still asleep. His longish light brown hair, his strong back and his wiry limbs. I almost don't know who he is. A relative stranger, really, still such a new and unfamiliar presence, just like springtime in Portland.

In a few weeks, I will no longer be married to Paul. I will sell my wedding ring—a ruby set in a platinum band that was bought at an antique store in rural Maine—for a very small amount. I just want that part of my life to be over, erased, forgotten. I need to tell you that the ruby was cracked down the center. That always haunted me. Something about it made my marriage feel flawed, damaged.

It was flawed and damaged, but I didn't know it at the time.

I will be in downtown Portland with Drew when I sell the ring for a hundred dollars cash. He won't understand my mood because he's never been married one day and then not married another.

I don't even think he's been with someone for that long at all, not really. He had a girlfriend once. But then she left him for another guy just like I left another guy for him.

We used to work together, Drew and I, and now we are lovers. It happened fast and wouldn't stop, even though I had no intention of leaving Paul. I was working for Drew, and then we were making out at his house. Now we spend hours with our hands all over each other.

I'm upending my life by choosing him. It feels like those golden flowers are drawn to us. The branches are getting twisted into a wild mass, just like we are.

I get out of bed and go into the kitchen to make coffee.

As I walk down the hallway, the old floorboards creak. In many ways, I don't know where I am. But I do know that I want to be here, that I need to be here.

What I don't know yet is that I will stay.

I put the kettle on to boil and grind the coffee.

Then I crawl back into bed and wrap myself around Drew. I put my face into the back of his neck, and I feel both hope and fear. I know that this is a risk. I know that this is not a committed relationship, like the one that I have chosen to abandon.

But I can't help it. It seems beyond my control, even though I have allowed it to happen.

We sip coffee together in bed, with the cream and the sugar, with the love and the lust.

It's the first sunny day in months. The last time it was sunny, I was living with my husband and our cat. It was late summer, and we were new to Portland, so wide-eyed and hopeful.

We had no idea what was to come; we had no idea what was to come apart.

It's late Saturday morning, the whole day ahead of us. Drew cleans up the breakfast dishes, eggs and toast and fruit. We get a little stoned over more coffee, then sit on the back patio with the sun warming our faces. I can hardly believe how good the warmth feels. Drew is on his back with his eyes closed.

I walk into the backyard in bare feet and snap a few branches off the shrub, put them into a jar of water on the kitchen table.

I am staking my claim at this old, weathered house that isn't mine—not yet.

We bike a few miles down to Southeast Portland. I'm on a vintage green three-speed and Drew is on an old black single-speed. We stop at a thrift store and lock up the bikes. We look through bins of vinyl, showing each other dated cover graphics and laughing. Drew buys an old book about typesetting and another about graphic design of the 1960s. I buy each of us a ceramic coffee mug. Mine is small and round and speckled light blue. Drew's is dark brown and chunky.

I could stay in this shop forever, looking at all the old things, still a little stoned and over-caffeinated, feeling as if I am lost in another era, one where I wasn't in my twenties and fucking up my life.

I secure our thrift finds in my bike basket, nesting the mugs in my hoodie so they don't break. We ride a few blocks to visit a friend of Drew's. He likes to stop in on people, unannounced. I would never do that. We grew up on different coastlines, in different cultures. I sit on a tattered velvet couch on the porch, while Drew knocks on the door. Ashtrays are spilling over with cigarette butts and empty beer cans and glasses take up most of a small, wooden coffee table. Brian, a tall guy with short, messy blond hair, comes out in brown polyester pants, an old t-shirt and bare feet. A cat with long gray and white hair follows him onto the porch.

Brian sits on a rickety wooden chair, lights a cigarette, and sips on black coffee in a chipped mug. He runs a small record label and he and Drew talk about some local bands. I don't know the bands, so I don't engage in the conversation. I pet the cat. The sun feels good, and I am content sitting on the musty couch, kind of listening to Brian and Drew, but not really caring about what they are saying. I feel a sudden sense of freedom, because I am so far away from my family and my friends.

I am no longer with my husband.

I'm three thousand miles away from the person that I used to be.

We smoke a little pot out of a small glass bong and then I feel like leaving. I want to get back on my bike, so I can watch Portland go by in a muted, technicolor light. I want to get back into bed with Drew, where all time comes to a stop and everything that is hard, scary, and tiring melts away.

We cycle through the neighborhood with the large Craftsman homes and the tidy front lawns with the kids and the dogs and the old money. We stop at a park and sit on a hill with our bikes propped against a big tree. People seem to be outside for the first time since winter. The ground is a little wet and the air is a little cool, but the sun is warm.

I lay my head on Drew's lap and close my eyes while he looks up at the sky.

Around 6 p.m.: the apartment is warm, clean, well-lit, pleasant. I make it that way, energetically, devotedly (enjoying it *bitterly*): henceforth and forever, I am my own mother.

—Roland Barthes

After I became a mother I learned
that I am a woman, and after that,
I learned what people think of
women. It happened very fast.

—Sarah Manguso

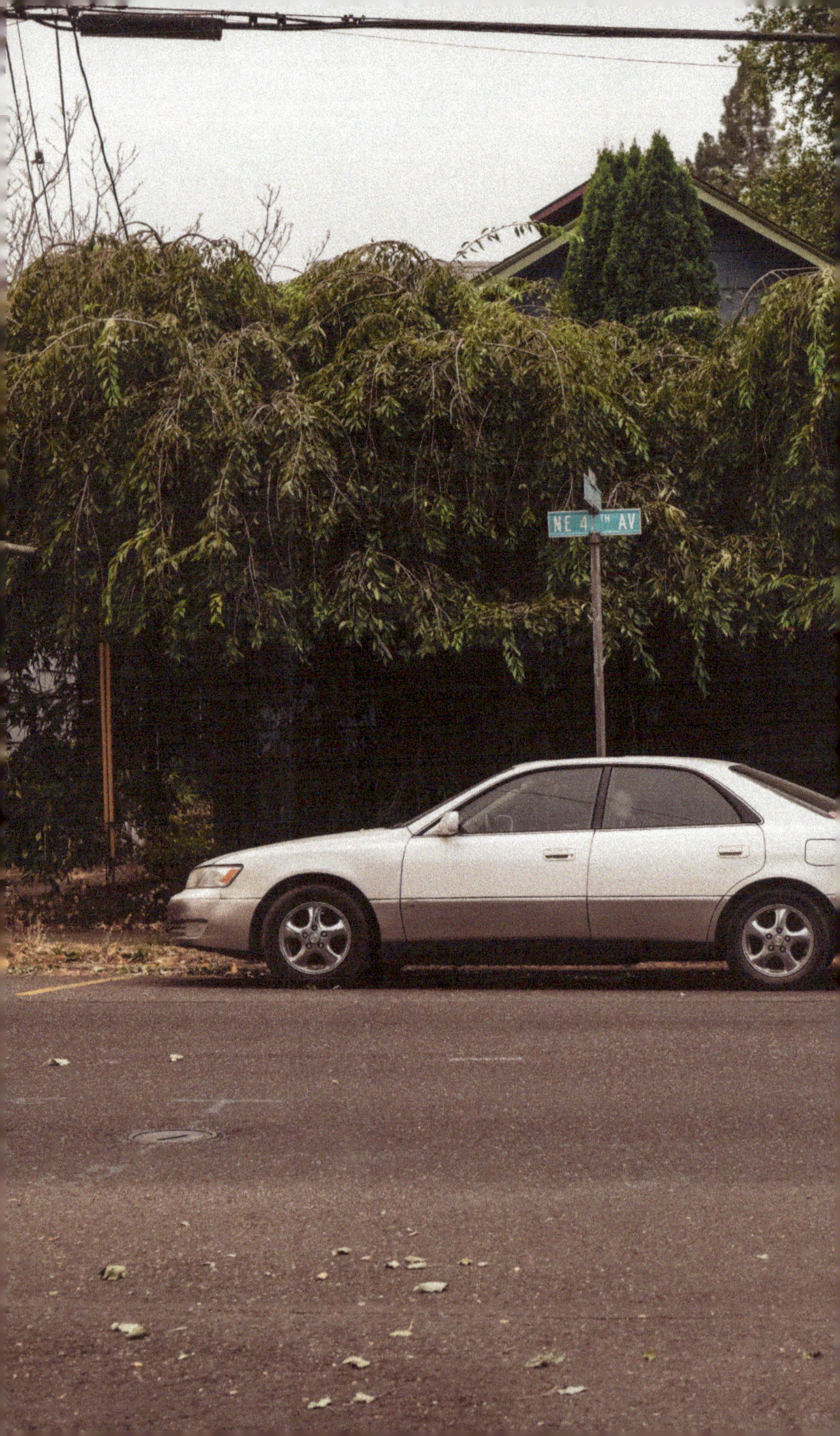
NE 4TH AV

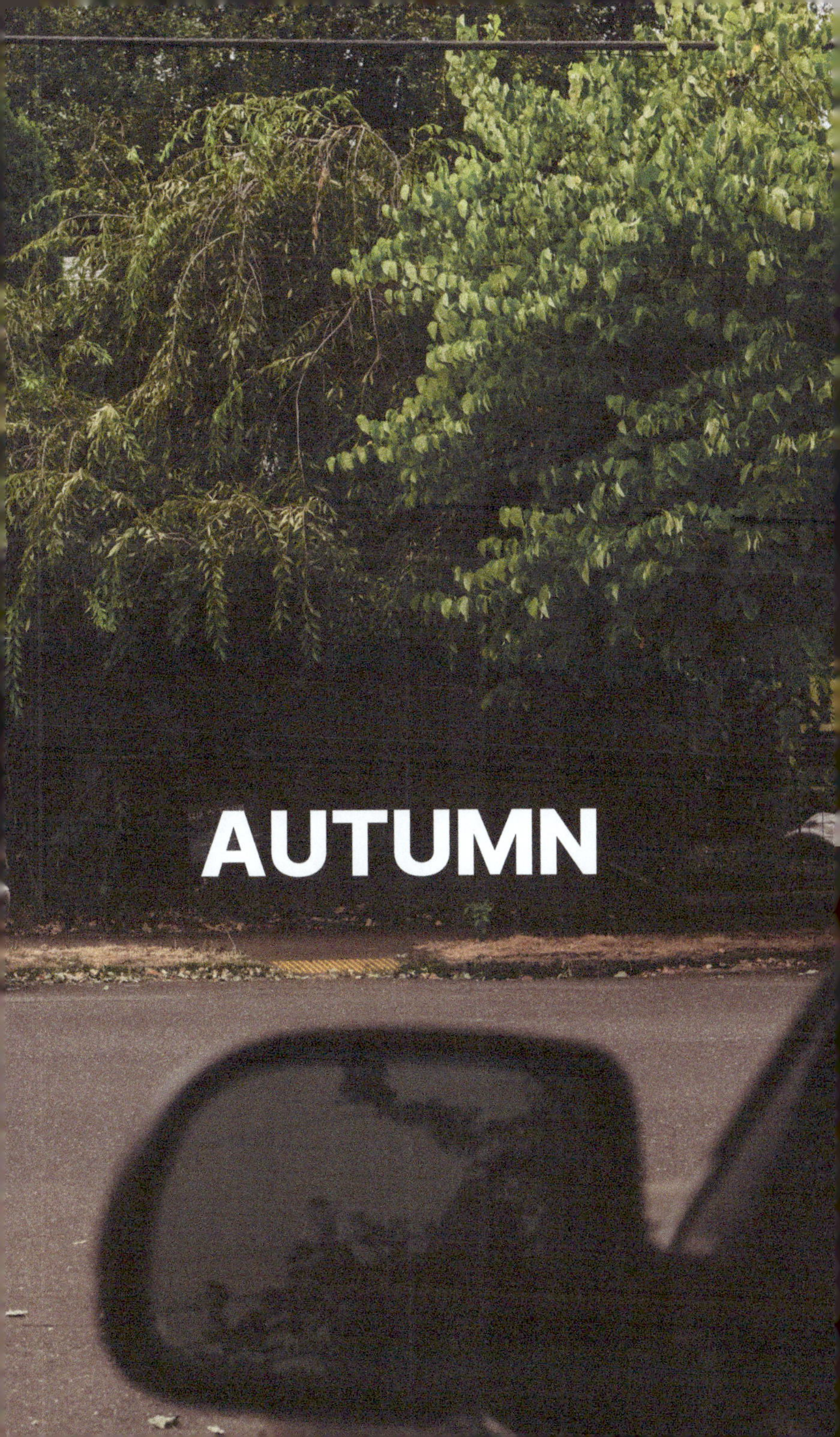
AUTUMN

The house is finally quiet, tidied.

In the early mornings, before the sun is up and while the house is still cast in that blue-gray light, Ana often finds herself standing in the middle of the kitchen in disbelief at the person that she has become.

She is no longer anxious, fearful, and debilitated.

And she knows that in just a few years, Lucien will be moved out of the house, on his own, launched. For now, she wakes up and fixes him breakfast, makes sure he gets off to school on time. She dotes on the boy, which makes Drew bristle because she doesn't dote on Drew.

Ana makes her son morning tea like her own mother made her morning tea. She serves him avocado toast with sliced apple on the side. There is both a sense of duty and a sense of satisfaction in the caregiving, because she knows that the boy's adult self will benefit from her care.

> "You don't have to do this, you know," Lucien said to Ana a few months ago.

It was an early morning before school, and he must have been in a teen mood. She chose not to respond. He hasn't said anything like that to her again.

Despite the morning tea, the care that Ana got as a child was inconsistent, chaotic, and at times, smothering. And yet, Ana knows that she did benefit from the special gestures that her mother offered her, because a lot of what Ana offers to Lucien she learned from her mother.

You can tell that Drew did not receive this kind of care, because he doesn't offer it to Ana and Lucien. When Ana does offer it to him, he doesn't know how to reciprocate. She used to think that Drew didn't care, but she has since come to learn that he doesn't know how to care.

It was modeled for Ana, but it was never modeled for Drew.

Drew and Lucien have just left on their bikes. Ana loads the dishwasher, wipes the counters, sweeps up the kitchen and then the bathroom. She walks the dog and hatches a plan to go to a yoga class before getting to work on the writing.

But then she gets home and notices that they are low on milk. There is only one slice of usable bread left, tucked between the butt end pieces that nobody ever wants to eat unless Ana makes french toast out of them. She also needs to figure out something to make for dinner.

As she stands in the kitchen assessing her findings, feelings of resentment course through her body. It starts down at the feet, travels up the spine and ends with a top-of-the-head ball of heat. Ana remembers one of her yoga teachers calling this kundalini energy.

The other morning Ana watched as Drew poured himself a bowl of cereal, finishing the box and then placing the crinkly plastic and cardboard box into the recycling bin. As he cut up a banana, poured milk into the bowl, and started eating, she realized that not only were they now out of cereal (Lucien often ate cereal after school or before bed as a snack) but that Drew had no intention of procuring any more.

She knew that he wouldn't add it to a list of things they needed, nor would he ask if Ana would be going to the store soon. He just drank his coffee and ate his cereal and went about his day.

"It doesn't matter to you, so you don't make any changes," Ana said to Drew a few weeks prior.
"But I made dinner the other night," he responded.
"I got the food and told you what to do and then you cooked it!" she snapped back.

It's the same conversation they've been having for over ten years, ever since Lucien was born. Prior to becoming a mother, Ana was too lost and stoned to worry about who had gone grocery shopping, who had cleaned the bathroom or who had walked the dog.

These types of domestic things didn't matter to her yet and she is continually surprised that they matter so much to her now. Once another human being that requires looking after is in the mix, you really start keeping tabs.

It was a seismic shift for Ana, this mothering.

When she first hooked up with Drew, Ana didn't know what to look for in a partner. She had just left a very brief marriage because she fell in love with Drew by accident.

It wasn't rational; she wasn't rational.

During their early years together, Ana and Drew smoked and drank their childhood traumas away so by the time Lucien came along, everything that had been swept under the carpet began to creep up to the surface. Having a child will do that to you.

Eventually, she would find a therapist who she couldn't manipulate into thinking she was fine, that she just needed to brainstorm some silly life ideas. Ana needed someone who could help her look at the core of her wounds, otherwise she would just continue to skirt around them. She has come to learn how important it is to find the taproot, otherwise you just end up wallowing in the mud.

And in time, she would also stop filling her head with wine and weed.

Where she began to turn towards the ick, Drew continued to turn away from the ick. Just like she made the choice to look at it through a microscope, he made the choice to keep the blindfold on, to put the mirror away.

We get to make that choice, she realized in time, after trying for so many years to push his nose into the pile of shit. Not everyone makes the choice to excavate the detritus of their pasts. It can be extremely uncomfortable and not everyone is resourced enough.

We get to choose. Either we look or we don't want to see.

Ana sits at the kitchen table with her phone and makes a shopping list.

She will go to the store, and then she'll take the noon yoga class and write at a cafe for a few hours before she picks up Lucien from school. She feels a little better with a plan set, the tightness dissipating.

Another side effect of an unstable childhood is that she feels much safer when she has control of a situation.

> During the weekdays, she would be left alone with her mother. She would be sent to her father's house on the weekends. Her mother had a decent job, and she wasn't out partying or anything, that wasn't the issue—it's that her mother wasn't able

to manage money, nor was she fit to raise a child on her own. She would get paid on a Friday and would cash her paycheck and spend all of it over the weekend, sometimes not paying the bills that needed to be paid or not buying enough groceries to get them through the following week.

When we are raised in this type of environment, Ana has since learned, the shit feelings that we experienced as a kid tend to crop back up. When Ana sees that the food is low, she feels scared and out of control, and then the feelings that she had towards her mother are directed towards Drew.

He ignores the situation like her mother ignored the situation.

Ana grabs a few shopping totes from behind the door, gets into the car and drives to the grocery store. While she is driving, she is suddenly overcome with guilt, thinking how she should have biked.

At the store, she buys oranges from South America, kiwis from New Zealand, bananas from Mexico. She feels terrible because she vowed to buy only seasonal, locally-sourced produce. She gets a ball of guilt in her stomach as she puts her debit card into the machine, wishing that she could just go back in time and do this all over again.

Ana thanks the checkout person and leaves, practically in tears, feeling like an eco-failure. She gets home, puts the groceries away and then heads up to a cafe on Northeast Alberta Street.

The sun is finally peeking out after a lengthy spell of chilly rain. She arrives a few minutes early to pick up Lucien, so Ana parks her bike at the racks and sits down on a wooden bench in the middle of the concrete schoolyard. She attempts to hide behind her sunglasses, earbuds in, looking down at her phone, hoping to avoid conversation.

When she's gone deep into the writing, she feels too spun out for schoolyard small talk. When Lucien was a bit younger, Ana enjoyed sitting with the other parents near the playground after school while the kids played or stopping off at the park across the street from the school and sitting on a blanket in the grass. It was some of the only adult time she got besides her time at home with Drew and it was both welcome and appreciated.

There's one parent, the father of a child in Lucien's grade, who always wants to talk to her because he's working on a novel. Ana avoids him like she avoids the PTA moms, who are always begging for favors. She laughs a little to herself thinking how there is nothing worse than a man working on a novel when you are trying to be lost in your own head.

More and more people gather in the schoolyard, mostly worn-out mothers tethered to whiny toddlers or babies strapped to their chests but also some haggard-looking bearded dads and a few gray-haired grandparents. When Lucien entered kindergarten six years ago, the school was predominately Black kids. Now it's predominately white. When Ana moved into the neighborhood in the early aughts, there was one coffee shop and two Mexican restaurants. Now there's an artisanal ice cream parlor and a bakery where they grind their own grains.

The bell rings and a swarm of kids comes spilling out of the doors. After a few moments, Ana sees Lucien. When he was younger, he would run and jump on her but now he saunters towards her casually.

"Hey, Ma," Lucien says.

"Hi, my sweetheart," Ana says, kissing him on his head.

She stands up, grabs his backpack, and puts it into her bike basket while the boy unlocks his bike from the rack. And then they ride together through the park. She rings her bell at some neighbors who are with their younger children.

That used to be me, she thinks to herself.

When they get home, Ana makes Lucien a toasted bagel with cream cheese and brings it into the living room. She is suddenly overcome with shame again.

She thinks about the mothers who bake banana bread and sit at the kitchen with their children after school, helping them with homework. Ana lets her child watch mindless shows on Netflix so she can read The New Yorker and look at her phone, texting friends back east about how much Portland sucks when it rains.

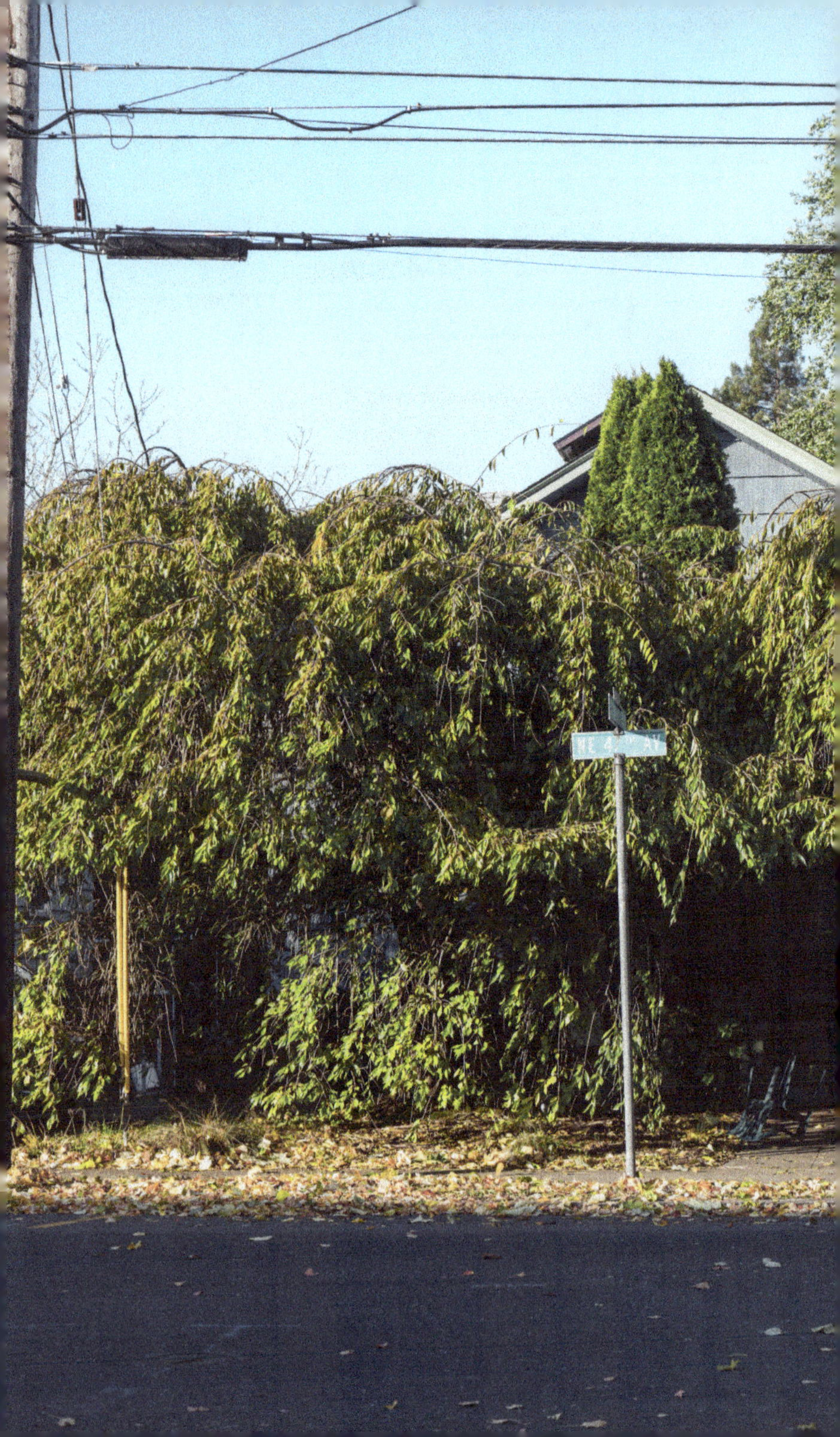
NE 4 TH AV

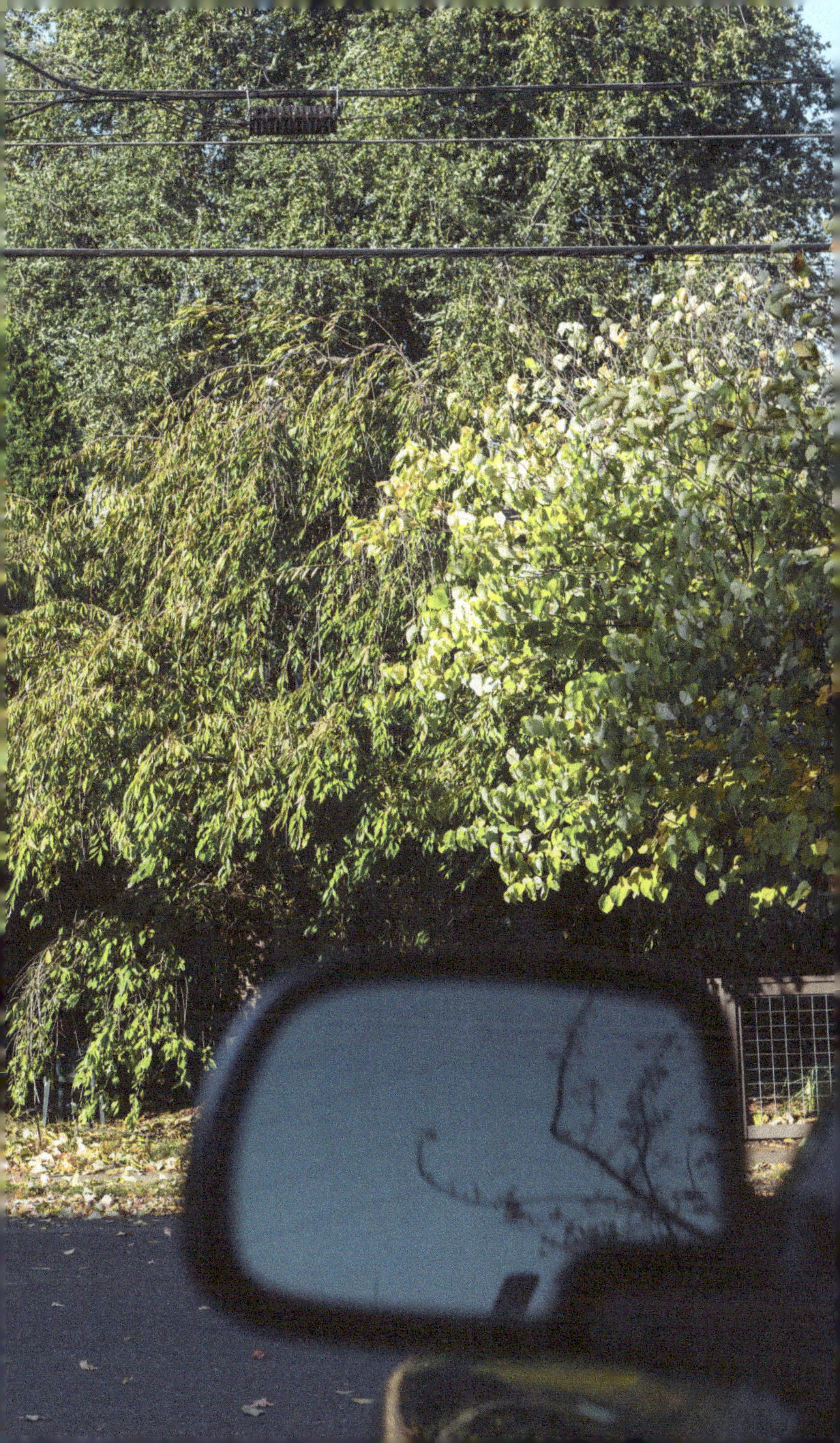

It's early evening and Ana makes pan-fried dumplings, brown rice and an omelet for Drew and Lucien to have for dinner. She rarely goes to evening yoga classes, but she has plans to meet a friend there. They'll have tea afterward.

Ana sets the table, leaves the food on the stove, and tells her family that she'll be home around nine.

"Okay, hon, have fun," Drew says.
"Can you make sure that Lucien has a shower after dinner?"
"But I had one last night!" Lucien fires back from his room.
"No, that was two nights ago," Ana says. "Sorry."
"Okay, fine," Lucien says.

The autumn air feels cold and heavy in her lungs as she rides her bike through the park. She pedals fast and hard through the dark, releasing the tensions of a householder's life: the incessant tidying of the home, the constant caregiving, the nagging feeling of never being off duty.

Ana arrives at the yoga studio, locks up her bike and checks in at the front desk. She collects two sets of props: mats, straps, blankets, bolsters. It's a gentle yoga class, so there will be lots of stretching and long, easy poses.

Ana feels restless.

She sits upright with closed eyes but keeps opening her eyes and craning her neck, looking out for her friend. As the room fills, she notices other pairs of people chatting. Her friend arrives right before the teacher comes into the studio. Ana is anxious and wants to chat with her friend, but she knows that the class is due to start any moment.

They smile at each other and then settle into a seated meditation pose.

Throughout class, Ana squints her eyes when the teacher asks the students to keep them shut. She often compares her postures to other people's postures. If her friend takes a pose to the deepest extent, then she tries to do the same even though it might be a strain, going against one of the golden rules of yoga.

At the end of the class, everyone chants as a group. Ana does not chant as loud as she would like, because she is afraid to be heard, especially by her friend who doesn't chant at all. Ana always thinks that her voice will sound terrible and tone-deaf, even though she loves to sing and has always dreamed about being the lead singer in a band.

When it's time to roll up the mat, to put away the props and exit the studio, Ana is one of the first to get up and leave the room. She quickly tells her friend that she will meet her at the cafe. Ana avoids eye contact and hopes that the teacher is not near the exit so she doesn't have to thank her for class.

She rushes outside successfully not having to say anything to anyone.

Ana bikes to the cafe, about a ten-minute ride down darkened, quiet backstreets.

Modest bungalows are lit up for the evening and there is a chill in the air, a benign drizzle. Ana feels good after a relaxing yoga class and looks forward to a warm cup of tea and a chat with her friend, whom she initially met at a yoga retreat in Mexico the previous year. Everyone in the group got sick with a stomach bug except for Ana and her friend, something that they share a sense of pride about, as if they are somehow superior.

It's warm and moderately busy inside the tea shop and it feels comforting to come in from the dark, wet evening. A few people are huddled together on the two vintage couches, chatting intimately. The rest are slumped over laptops. Ana claims a small table near the window. She sees her friend walking back from the counter.

"I ordered some mint tea for us," her friend says.
"Okay, sounds great."

Ana knows that she comes off as grounded, contained, satisfied.

What most people don't know about Ana, what she doesn't expose, is that she exists in a quiet, sustained state of psychic and physical pain. What she doesn't share is that she often thinks that there must be a better place to live, that she could have a better home, that there might be a more suitable partner for her. How maybe she could be with someone who would be willing to hear what she had to say, who would see her and who would actually know her.

Ana and her friend sit across from each other, sipping tea and talking about how Portland has changed over the past few years. How there are all these "local" chain businesses and how sterile and capitalistic everything has become.

They both moved to Portland when things were still sleepy, vintage, and cheap.

"Last week, I overheard someone talking about single-origin espresso!" Ana tells her.
"You know, I think a lot of people work in tech remotely now," her friend says.
"I bet they live in those new condo buildings and have designer doodle dogs," Ana says, and they both laugh.

Whenever Ana has these kinds of conversations, she just ends up feeling bad about herself. She shouldn't be so shallow and judgmental, she thinks. She should find deeper ways to connect. But sometimes the only way that she connects to people is talking about other people. Rather than talk about how she herself is really feeling.

"So, what's been going on?" her friend asks, as they wind down their visit.
"Oh, just focused on Lucien, his school stuff, and writing," Ana says.
"How's the writing going?" her friend asks.
"It's good, hard."
"And how's Drew?"
"He's okay. Just super busy with work," she says.

They talk about getting together for dinner soon and then bring their teapot and cups to the counter. They hug outside the cafe.

Her friend turns the corner and Ana walks over to the patio to unlock her bike.

She feels shameful and awkward now that she is alone, thinking about how she probably said stupid, shallow things to her friend. Their conversation runs like a tape in her head. It's raining now. She unlocks her bike and rides home, feeling exhausted from the day and ready to take a hot shower and crawl into bed with a book.

When she walks into the house, soaking wet, the weight of everything hits her all at once. The kitchen is a mess, and all the lights are on. The dog swarms Ana for treats and she can hear that Lucien is still awake, watching shows on her laptop.

"Hey guys," she says, walking into the living room.
"Hey, Ma," Lucien says.
"Did you have a shower yet?" she asks him.
"Nah," he says.
"Yeah, sorry, we were just gonna' do that," Drew says, looking up at Ana and pretending that he wasn't looking at his phone.
"Seriously," she says, annoyed. "It's a school night."

Drew gets up and goes into the kitchen to clean up. Since Lucien still needs a shower, Ana will have to wait to take one herself. She's chilled to the bone and her clothing is wet from the ride home.

"C'mon, man," she says to Drew when Lucien goes into the bathroom and shuts the door.

"What?" Drew asks, defensively.

"I asked you to make sure Lucien had a shower before I got home."

"Sorry, I didn't realize what time it was," he says.

Ana changes into dry clothes and helps Drew clean up the kitchen. She makes the decision to let her anger go or else she knows it will escalate into an argument. She doesn't want to fight in front of Lucien. And she's too tired to get into anything with Drew because she knows that his hackles will go up and then he won't be able to hear her.

They would just talk-fight in circles.

When Lucien is out of the shower, he gets into his pajamas and sits at the kitchen table eating a bowl of cereal. Ana showers and gets into bed. Lucien comes in and they nuzzle their feet together.

"Make sure you brush your teeth," she says, still looking down at her book.

"Okay, Ma," he says and runs off to the bathroom.

Lucien comes back into Ana's bed and dozes off. Ana reads with the boy's warm, sleeping body next to her. She can hear Drew knocking around in the kitchen, putting dishes away. But she's still upset and doesn't want to engage with him.

After some time, she falls asleep with the lights on and the book on her chest.

They're at a vegetarian restaurant on Northeast Alberta Street talking about who will watch Lucien in a few weeks, as both of them will be out of town at the same time. Ana has a friend's birthday weekend at the coast and Drew has a work trip down to Santa Cruz.

A server comes over to refill their coffee. They both look up at her and smile.

Ana used to frequent this restaurant when Lucien was a baby, when she didn't want to sit at home. Sometimes she would sketch out scene ideas in a journal, as if someday she would have the bandwidth to write a book.

She recalls one time that she was having lunch in a large booth and noticed two former advertising agency colleagues by the front door. The restaurant was full, so they had to wait for a table. Lucien was an infant at the time, sleeping in his car seat next to Ana in the booth. She awkwardly waved the colleagues down and invited them to join her. They still worked together, so they caught her up on agency gossip.

One of them had a child about a year older than Lucien but ended up going back to work a few months after the child was born. Ana didn't plan to go back to work, not in advertising at least. Like Ana, this woman's spouse stayed home with the child.

"He definitely has the harder role," she told Ana.
"Really?" Ana asked.
"I get to catch up on emails and take long lunches," she said, smiling.

Ana thought about what it would be like if she had gone back to work full time and Drew had stayed at home with Lucien. She immediately pictured a house in constant disarray, having to work full time and still doing a majority of the householding.

And the men would absolutely say that their job was more difficult.

Even though he never admits to it, Ana knows that Drew feels that his role is more challenging because he is responsible for most of their income. It shows in up many ways, mostly around his ambivalence towards the householding and caregiving. He will do things, he never pushes back if Ana asks him to do something, but he doesn't necessarily initiate.

It often feels like he is helping Ana, like an assistant. In time, Ana will come to understand that Drew believes that this is his role because of his gender.

The food arrives and again, they smile and thank the server.

"I can just ask my mom to come stay with Lucien," Drew says between sips of coffee.
"Are you being serious?" Ana snaps.

She reminds him of the last time they left his mother alone with Lucien—how the boy, who was then around six years old, hadn't been bathed for the five days they were away, and still wore the same clothes as the day they left. They had taken a quick trip down to Mexico and stayed at a lovely historic inn, lounging poolside and having daytime sex while their child was being neglected.

Ana reminds him that the house was a disaster, that their son and Drew's mother were both emotionally distraught and physically unkempt when they returned. She reminds Drew that his mother couldn't wait to leave as soon as they got home, how she left immediately, without even asking them about their trip.

"Some people just aren't the type to take care of kids," Ana says.
"You only look at the negative in things," Drew snaps back.

When Lucien was just a few months old, the three of them were struck with a terrible flu. Ana begged Drew to call and ask his mother to come help. She lives just a few hours drive away.

He hesitated, which she initially took as not caring. What Ana realized later, is that he knew that his mother wouldn't come.

Ana's own mother had passed away just a few months prior and not only was she sick with the flu, but she was also sleep-deprived and grief-stricken. Drew's mother was their only family within driving distance, and she assumed that, of course, a grandmother would come to their aid.

> "Tell Ana that she needs to learn how to do this on her own," she overheard her telling Drew over the phone.
> "Okay, Mom, we'll be fine," he told her.

Ana was crestfallen, so desperate for the help, in such need to be cared for, to be mothered. She wouldn't be fine. She remembers weeping in bed while nursing the baby—sick, scared, and vulnerable.

Ana had been ignorant in assuming that just because Drew had a mother who lived nearby, that she would be available to support them once the baby was born. This was when Ana realized that she would be truly alone in her experience of mothering.

She had Drew, of course she did, and she had lovely friends and tremendous privileges, but she didn't have her own mother and now she wouldn't have Drew's mother.

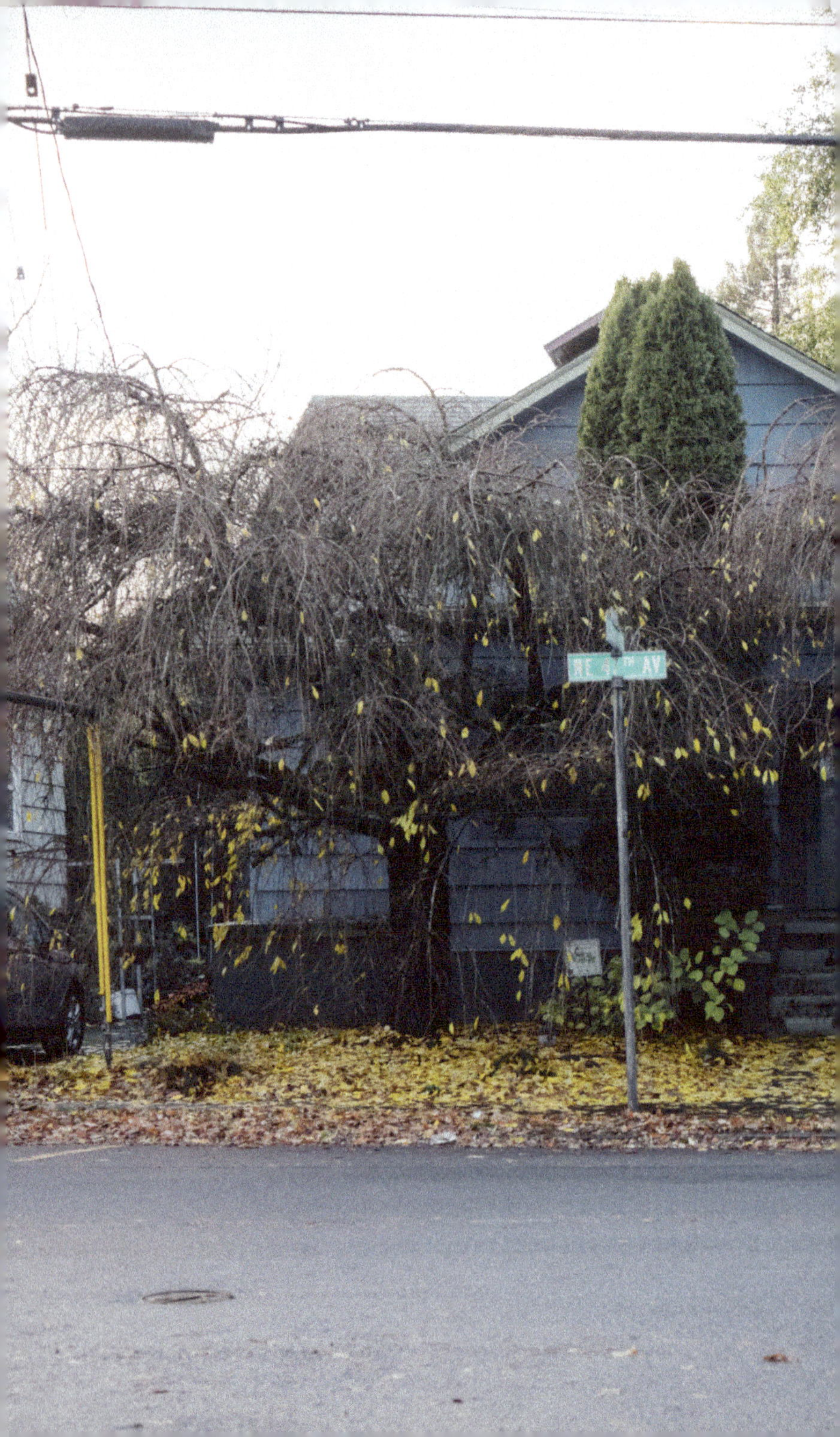
NE   AV

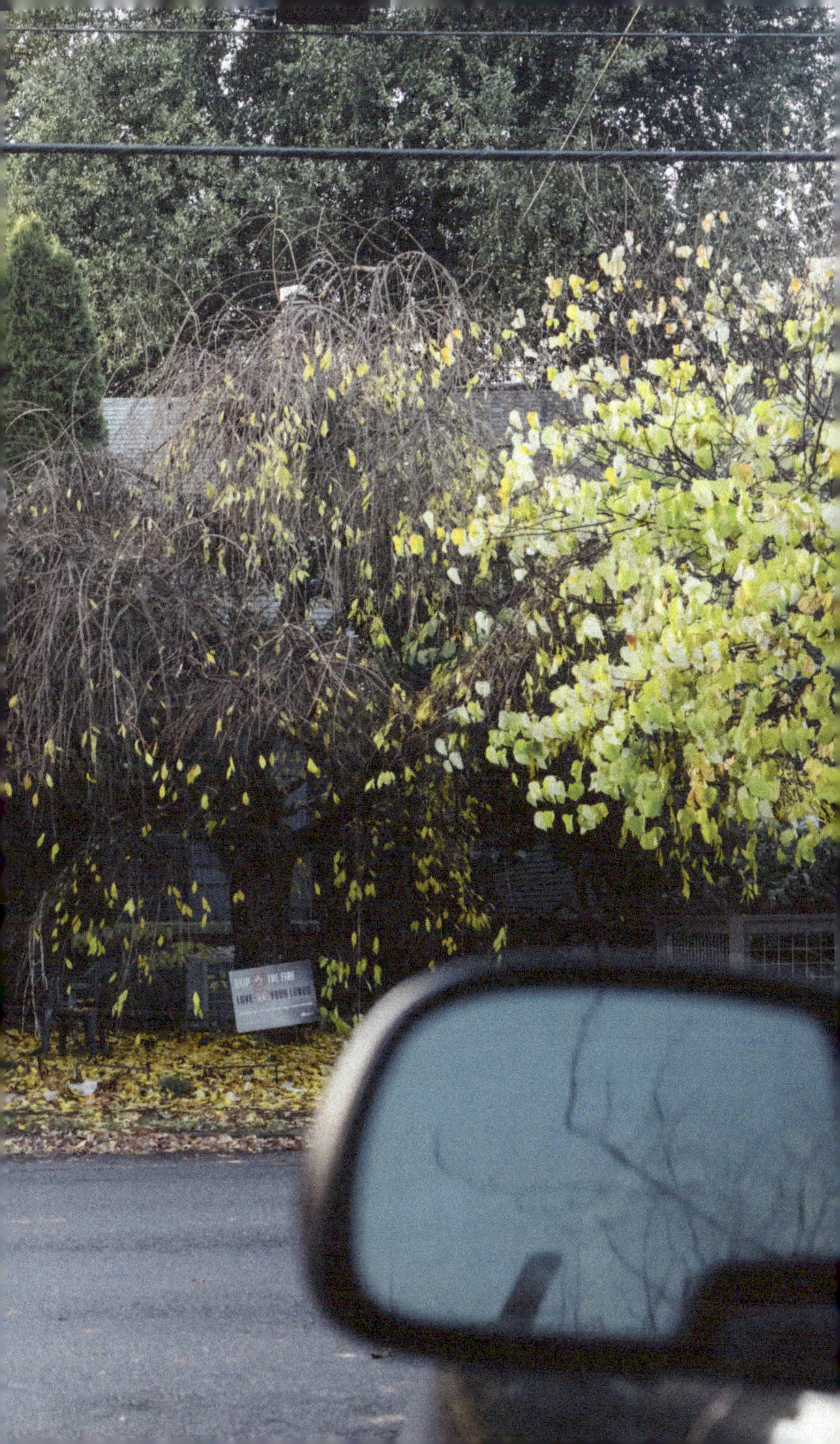
THE FIRE
LOVE YOUR LUNGS

Drew is standing at the stove boiling milk.

Ana gets the milk directly from a farm; it is raw and unpasteurized.

Drew makes fresh yogurt from the milk because it helps Ana's stomach heal from so many years of feeling anxious and afraid. To make the yogurt, you boil the milk to a certain temperature and then you cool the milk down to a certain temperature before adding in the yogurt culture.

She doesn't make it herself because she is certain she will fuck it up because she thinks that she fucks everything up. She fucked up her first marriage and she will probably fuck up this one too.

But then she remembers the one time that she did make the yogurt—it was thick and creamy. Drew's is thin and watery.

While Drew is stirring the mixture, Ana sits at the kitchen table. They are discussing their finances because Drew recently turned in their taxes. Ana pays the bills and buys the groceries with the money Drew makes as a freelance graphic artist.

Sometimes she takes herself out to lunch for twelve-dollar bowls of brown rice, kale, and black beans. She buys books and clothes for herself and the child. Drew doesn't spend the money he makes because he hardly buys anything at all. He wears old t-shirts that he's had for over a decade and gets pants at thrift stores and eats the food that Ana procures and cooks.

Over the past six months or so, Ana has siphoned almost three thousand dollars from their joint savings account. Drew hasn't given himself a raise in almost a decade. He refuses to acknowledge that the cost of living in Portland has gone up and that their expenses are a lot higher than they were before they had a child and now also, a second home.

"Hey, hon—I need some money deposited into our account," Ana says, nervously.
"What? Why?" Drew asks.
"Oh, it's just that I had to pay a bunch of extra bills this month," she says.
"Maybe I should take care of paying the bills!" Drew says in a firm tone.

Ana is holding four paperback books, because she was about to bring them out to her writing studio in the garage. Lucien is in his bedroom watching shows on her laptop. Ana looks at Drew, who is stirring the warm milk with one hand, and in the other hand is a long metal thermometer with a pointed tip.

She throws the books across the kitchen and into the dining room.

And then she goes into their bedroom and lays in a fetal position on the bed, weeping. After some time, Lucien walks in with the laptop, lays next to Ana, and continues watching his shows.

"It's no wonder you two found each other," Ana's therapist, Jayne, says.

"What do you mean?" Ana asks.

"Why don't you tell me what you think it means?" Jayne asks.

Jayne works out of a creaky room in an old Victorian house on a leafy street in southeast Portland, an elderly cattle dog at her feet. Ana sits on an overstuffed chair, cross-legged, hugging a cup of herbal tea.

She's been coming here for quite a few years now. There are times when it is painfully hard to excavate her past and there are days when it feels like a burden has been lifted.

When Jayne pokes the old, hard things, Ana often becomes distracted, dizzy.

"I feel funny," Ana says.

"Then we're really getting to something," Jayne says, smiling.

Ana would prefer to take this topic up later when she is alone, not while Jayne is staring at her from the other side of the room. She suddenly feels lazy and exhausted, ashamed that she can't answer Jayne's question. She feels as if she should know better by now, after years of paying all this money to Jayne for guidance.

"I don't know," Ana says, feeling like a stupid child. "I just don't know..."

"Yes, Ana. You do. Just take your time."

Ana sits with her eyes closed and struggles to figure things out. All she can think about is how she is not good enough, that she can't do what she is being asked to do.

She feels how it felt when a teacher would call on her as a kid in school when she didn't know the answer. She feels how it felt when her stepmother would yell at her for not doing something right.

"You are trying to think your way through this," Jayne says.
"I know..."
"Go more into your body," she tells Ana.
"I'm really trying," Ana says.
"I know you are," Jayne says, patiently.

Even though her eyes are closed, Ana can tell that Jayne is staring at her. She feels uncomfortable, unable to focus. She takes a deep breath and tries to feel her body. She feels her heart racing in her chest and there is a sensation of tightness in her stomach. She wants to open her eyes and talk about something else, sip tea, pet the dog.

"You found each other so you could heal from the traumas of your pasts," she finally says. "From your childhoods."

It always comes down to Jayne pointing out what Ana already knows. But she has so much fear and anxiety buried deep in her nervous system that she can't always get to the truth herself. She knows intuitively that both she and Drew had parents that were unfit in certain ways and that coming together as adults could enable them to work on themselves, to reparent themselves, together.

"But what if one of us is willing to look into the past and the other one isn't?" Ana asks.
"Then the person who is willing to look is also able to heal," Jayne tells her. "And that person becomes a model for the other person."

They've revisited this many times before: how Ana has tried to get Drew to go to therapy, how they had tried couples counseling, and how none of it stuck. She even tried farming Drew out to a young male therapist, a Portland hipster who wore a sweater vest in his portrait photo—someone she thought he could find relatable, feel comfortable opening up to.

When he came back from his one and only session, Drew told Ana the guy said that he didn't really need therapy.

"He doesn't think you need to talk about the fact that your mother left you when you were four?"
"I didn't tell him about that," he told Ana.

Couples counseling was an even worse disaster. Drew told the therapist, an odd woman who wore knee-length wool skirts and thick stockings with high-heeled shoes out of the 1920's, that Ana made a habit of diagnosing his family members with mental health disorders.

Really, all she said was that his father and brothers were alcoholics, which they are.

They lasted two, maybe three sessions before Drew and the therapist teamed up against Ana.

When Ana's time is up with Jayne, she and the dog walk her out to the front porch. It's rainy and cold outside and all Ana can think about is going home and crawling into bed. She walks the few blocks to her car feeling ashamed.

Ana gets back home and takes to the couch in an exhausted daze.

She thinks about Drew and how he refuses to investigate his past. How she works so hard at being a more grounded person, constantly picking herself apart and attempting to put herself back together, but in a better way.

She knows that this is her choice, that she chooses to excavate but that so many people choose to keep everything buried.

A feeling of panic comes over Ana. She realizes she may reach a point of being unable to deal with Drew's stoner avoidance anymore. How she might end up leaving him, which would mean partially leaving Lucien. Ana knows she could never do that: leave him, leave them. She realizes that the panic actually has more to do with her own childhood fears, how she wasn't always cared for, looked after, and how the idea of not being with Drew anymore feels similar to how she felt as a child.

She falls asleep and then jolts awake, remembering that she needs to work on writing before Lucien comes home from school. Ana reminds herself that she often feels anxious after a therapy session and that it will soon pass, leaving her feeling even more grounded than before. She often equates this therapeutic phenomenon with climbing Mount Everest. How climbers must reach the first base camp to acclimate to the altitude. How they titrate up and down through the various camps until they are fully acclimated and ready to attempt the ascent. She loves watching climbing documentaries to bear witness to the extreme physical suffering and endurance.

Ana wonders what a good analogy for reaching the top of Everest would be for her, maybe that that she would be okay with the present. That she would be okay with whatever she is confronted with.

She packs up her computer and leaves the house.

It's one of those moody Pacific Northwest autumn days, intermittent clouds and sun, plus short bursts of light rain. She wears a hooded sweatshirt under Drew's old denim jacket, a canvas bag slung over her shoulder.

She heads through the park on foot, passing Lucien's school, up to the tea shop.

When Ana arrives at the cafe, the person ordering in front of her is asking many questions about the different teas on the menu; there are so many teas. The woman running the register is patient with the customer, but Ana is frustrated because she doesn't have a lot of time to spare. She is upset with herself for not being calm enough to just work alone in her garage studio instead of waiting in line with these needy people.

Finally, the customer finishes her order. The woman turns around and apologizes to Ana for taking so long.

"That's okay," Ana says, smiling.

Ana orders a chai and finds a seat on a big couch. She opens her laptop and begins to feel more grounded, like everything is going to be okay now.

She eavesdrops on a conversation happening at a table behind her. It's a woman with gray hair set in a bun, probably somewhere in her sixties. She wears long, flowing cotton skirts and is here all the time, acting as if this tea shop is her office. She sits at a small table by the window, across from a much younger man in wire-rimmed glasses and short, greasy, dark hair. The woman is talking a lot and the young man just sits there nodding his head and listening, not saying anything. It sounds like the woman is coaching him on marketing himself somehow. Ana can't really decipher what they are talking about, but the woman is leading the conversation.

There are a few people who are here pretty much all the time.

There's the woman with the gray bun and then there is this short, stocky, middle-aged man who wears khaki shorts even in winter. He is friendly in an odd, almost creepy way and is usually at the same table each time, but the woman with the gray bun is standoffish. They are both always on their laptops and phones conducting business matters. The man takes phone calls outside, but the woman just takes her calls inside the cafe and has no problem speaking loudly, as if she is alone in her own kitchen. And then there is a tall, fit man who reads spiritual books and writes in his journal. One time Ana witnessed an argument between him and the woman with the gray bun because she was speaking too loudly on her phone inside the cafe. Ana was on his side.

The milky hot chai arrives, and Ana is able to get into the writing. She often has a hard time getting herself to write, but once she starts, she feels a lot better about her overall sense of purpose. She finds writing to be difficult, torturous at times. Treating herself to a hot beverage always motivates her, like a baby who self-soothes with warm milk.

Ana looks up from her laptop and outside the window onto Alberta Street. There were a handful of years when she wanted to either move back to New York to be closer to family or move to a different neighborhood in Portland, but she is suddenly grateful—for once, where she lives feels in alignment.

There is a break in the rain and the woman with the gray bun and the greasy young man are out front saying goodbye to each other. They shake hands and he walks away. The woman comes back in, talking loudly on her phone.

Ana turns back to the writing.

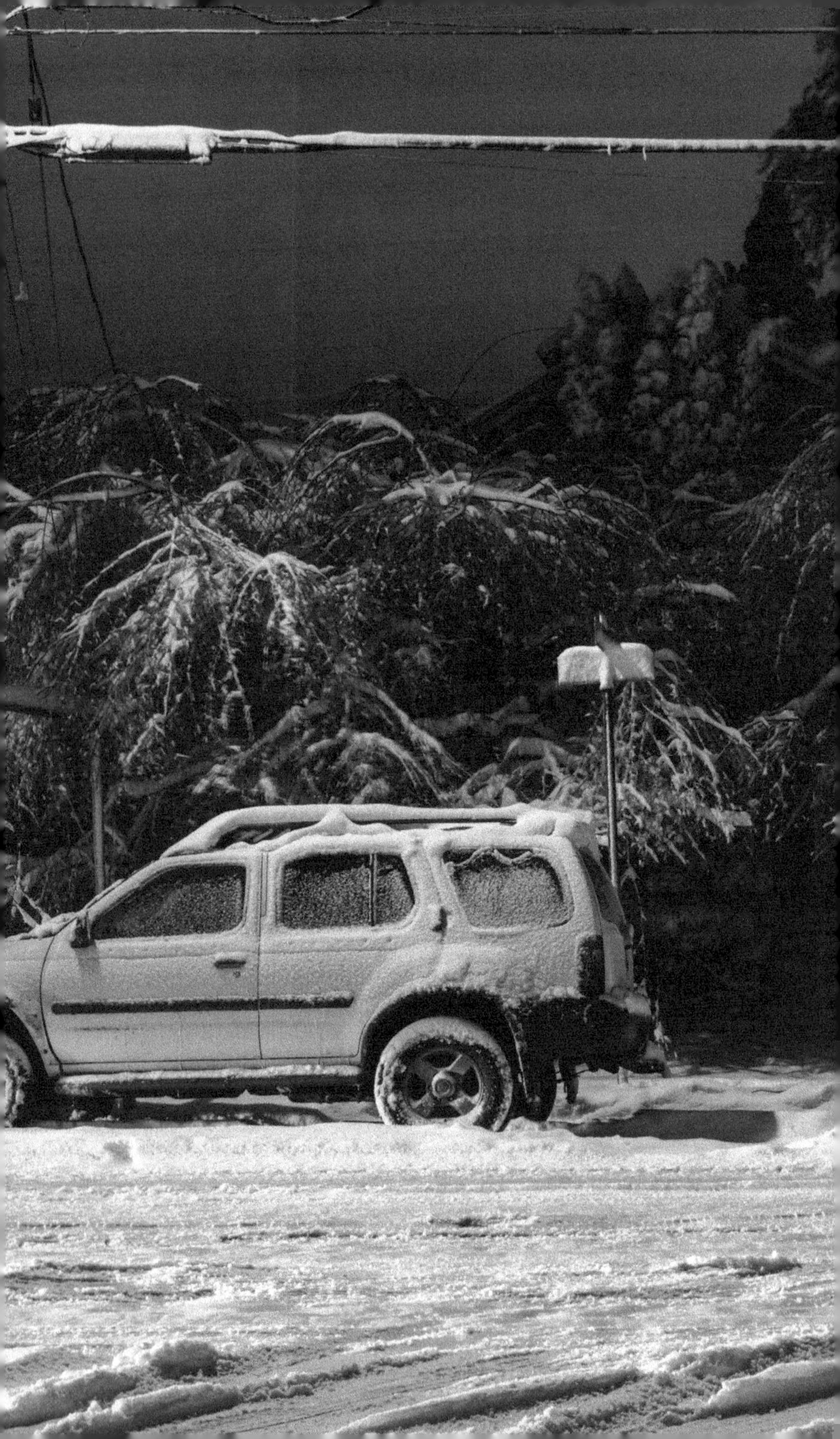

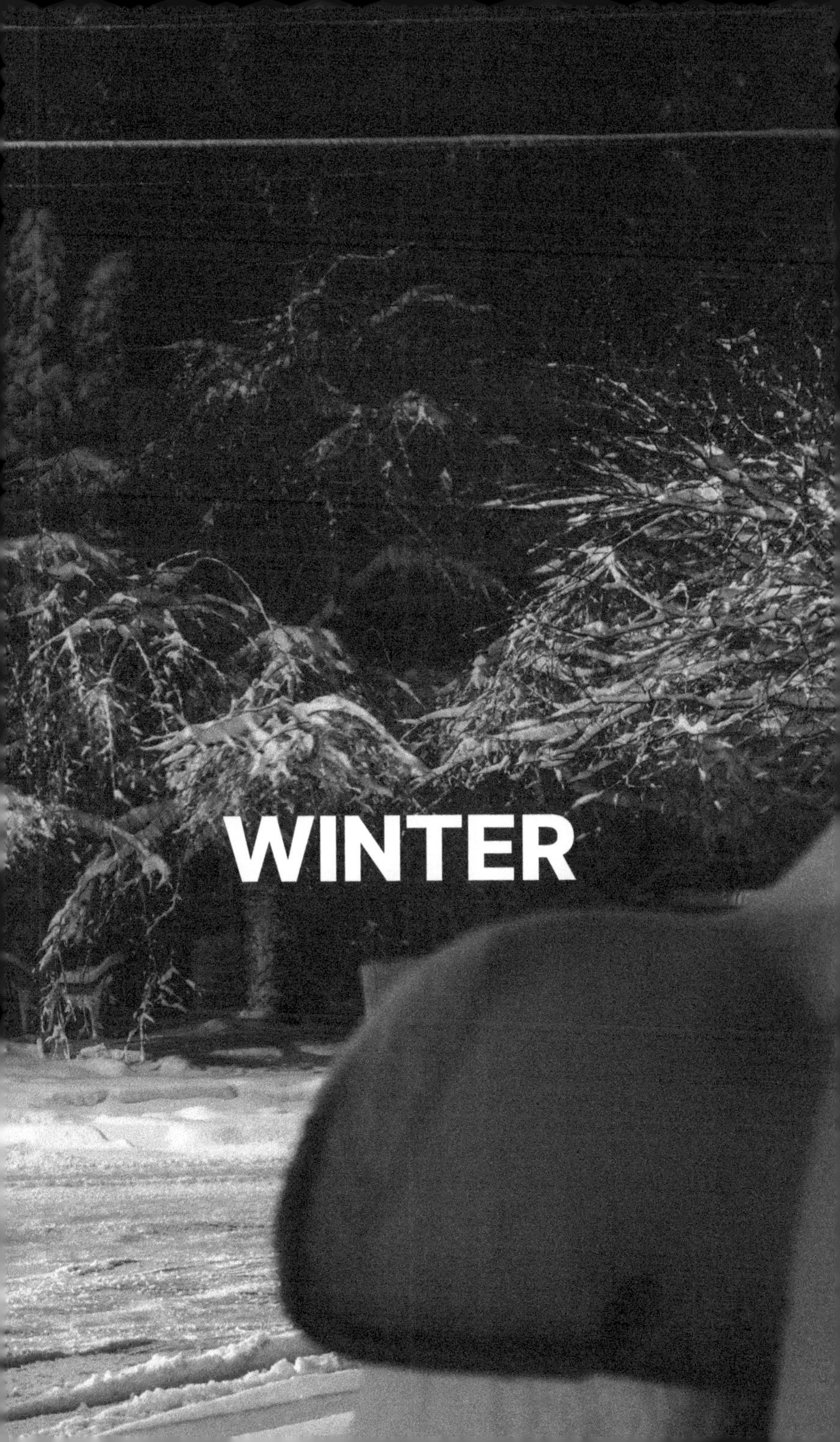

WINTER

It's late morning and a fire is raging in the wood stove of their cabin on the Northern Oregon Coast.

The air outside is crisp and clear, a break in the intermittent winter rain. Ana is sitting on the Eames lounger they inherited from Drew's family: well-worn black leather, missing buttons, creaky.

Next to Ana is a bookshelf that she likes to admire, a well-curated stack of literary anthologies, essay collections, and vintage books on camping, sauna, and weather. She thinks about how she would like to make a book someday, the kind of book that she would place on this shelf.

Ana likes to think about someone picking up her book, reading a few pages, and then putting it down to think, like a book of poetry.

Notebook and pen are splayed out on her lap. She closes the notebook and grapples with the fact that she needs to wash the breakfast dishes and then take the child and the dog down to the beach before cabin fever sets in.

But she doesn't want to move from her perch by the fire. As much as there is a tug to move, there is also a pull to stay.

Sometimes Ana thinks about what it would be like to take to bed for the day.

A friend once told her that when she feels the need to restore, she closes the blinds in her bedroom and spends a full day under the duvet. Ana knows she could never do that, not anymore at least.

She used to spend entire days getting stoned and watching multiple arthouse movies in a row. That was before. Before she had a family, and all of its responsibilities.

Now it seems like there is always something or someone that requires tending. Ana also feels that because she doesn't make a significant income, she needs to earn her keep in other ways.

Ana gets up from the chair and walks into the small galley kitchen with the wooden countertops and open shelving that Drew made from repurposed floorboards. She grabs a ceramic mug and a tea bag from the canister, fills the kettle with water, sets it on the stove to boil.

Hearing wet bamboo smacking gently against the windows, she peers outside and watches the tall fir trees cascade back and forth into one another. The weather has shifted to wind and rain, which means that her walk down to the beach may need to be postponed. Lucien will complain too much, and the dog will get too wet.

She hears Drew rustling in bed. He's been lounging, looking at his phone all morning. Lucien is still upstairs in the loft watching shows.

Ana finishes washing the dishes, wipes the counters, then pours the hot water for her tea, the dog circling her feet.

She takes back up in the chair by the fire, pulls out her notebook, sketches a few ideas. But then Ana remembers that Lucien has been on screens all morning and now Drew is out of bed, clearly pining to go surfing.

From across the room, she watches Drew look down at his phone. He paces around the living area, then goes into the kitchen and rinses out his coffee cup, puts it in the rack to dry.

He walks over and stands next to Ana by the fire, staring out the front window.

"What's going on, hon?" Ana asks Drew.
"Nothing...just looking at the waves," he says.

They broke ground on the cabin before Lucien was born and they finished construction when he was still a baby. There was a brief period when they would come out to the structure under construction and the three of them would sleep on camp mats with sleeping bags amidst the sawdust and piles of tools and materials.

It was a terrible time for Ana.

She was still so deep in grief from the loss of her mother and the cabin needed so much work and money to make it even semi-livable.

She loved Lucien more than anything, of course she did—there was so much joy and bliss in the mothering, but there was also so much pain from the recent mother-loss.

It would take many years to begin the process of healing.

It also took Ana a long time to bond with the house, because its conception had represented a very difficult time in her life. There was a lot of stress in rushing to complete construction, so they could refinance and get a mortgage. Ana and Drew had built the cabin on equity from their home in Portland, which had gone up in value considerably. But as much as Drew made a decent income, all their resources went into the housebuilding.

At one point, they only had twenty dollars remaining in their checking account. Multiple credit cards were maxed out, the high-interest debt compounding. What started out as an affordable parcel of scrubby rural land on the far edge of the continent—which Drew bought with his own savings before they were even married—had become a full-blown second home.

Most Fridays, Ana would muster up the energy to plan meals and procure groceries, then pack the car with the dog and the baby. They would plan their travels around Lucien's naps so it wouldn't mess up his sleep schedule.

Inevitably, there would be a few hours before leaving when Ana would get extremely testy and anxious, often exploding on Drew. She was worn out with getting everything and everyone ready to go and it always seemed that Drew just showed up when it was time to leave.

"We don't need to bring much," he would always say.
"Well, you don't need to bring much, but we have a baby, and we all need to eat for three days,"

What a wreck Ana was back then.

These weekend trips to the coast had become reminiscent of the Friday transitions from her mother's ramshackle apartment to her father's suburban home and back to the crappy apartment on Sunday evening again. Ana was destabilized just like when she was a kid.

After the cabin was completed, Drew was so thrilled about finally having a place near the ocean where he could surf and putter around in the yard. But Ana couldn't appreciate it, not yet. She doesn't know if he ever came out and told her so directly, but she knew that he thought she should just appreciate what they had and that there was nothing to complain about. If anything, Ana should be grateful, not everyone had a cabin at the coast.

It felt as if he looked away from her struggles, from their struggles. He couldn't face them. He wasn't a bad person; he just wanted everything to be okay.

It was also because Drew was totally fine, so Ana could sense that he felt there was nothing to really worry about. He still had the same job that he had before Lucien was born and he still slept through the night, while Ana was often roused by Lucien's cries and couldn't settle back down because her nervous system stayed on such high alert.

Ana doesn't know how long this cycled, but early motherhood still feels close. Even now, she feels guilty for not being resilient enough.

She sweeps the floors, burns some sandalwood incense, puts on an album. This is how she feels secure; there is a soothing sense of control that comes with order and cleanliness.

> "In a little bit, let's walk down to the beach, okay?" she yells up to Lucien.
> "Okay, Ma," he says.
> "I'm gonna head out for a surf, that cool, hon?" Drew asks Ana.
> "Please don't ask me for permission," she snaps. "Just go, it's fine."
> "I'll make dinner later," he says.

Ana knows that Drew won't make dinner later or that if he does, he will need her direction. He doesn't even know what she planned or what groceries they have.

She also feels a bit sad that she can't just run off and go surfing with Drew like she used to, in the pre-parenting beforetimes. When she had the energy to pull on a wetsuit and float in the cold Pacific. Ana loved surfing for a few years. That is, until she got spooked: one time she was held under a wave for a long time, came up gasping and shaking.

When she became a mother, she mostly gave up surfing. It was too risky, and required too much energy that she no longer had.

Drew leaves and then soon after, the child climbs down from the loft.

Ana sits with a book at the kitchen table, finishing her lukewarm tea, one leg tucked under the other, the same way her mother used to sit.

Ana recalls a winter afternoon when Lucien was just a baby. She walked down to the beach while Drew was out surfing a few miles south.

It was damp and wet outside and she had the baby bundled up in one of those jogging strollers with the burly tires. They kept that stroller in the shed for years: it was purple and stained with mud and mold, a Craigslist purchase. She had been trying to get the baby to nap so she could get time to read, maybe even get a little stoned and enjoy the landscape.

The lack of a proper night's sleep had become unbearable. Ana was shelled; she was a shell of a person.

And she believed that it was her own fault, like if she could just get herself back to sleep after nursing then she would be okay again. Like there was something fundamentally wrong with her that she couldn't just cozy up with the baby and fall asleep like the earth mamas in the books.

The unpaved road leading down to the beach is craggy and lined with potholes. You pass a few houses on both sides of the road, and then you go down a hill, over a creek bed, and turn left towards the ocean. You follow a narrow path covered in woodchips, which are often overgrown with native plants and in some seasons, they may be sprinkled with colorful wildflowers.

You reach a grassy overlook, where you can see two giant rocks jutting out of the feral Pacific and then it's another short, somewhat steep and oftentimes slippery path down to the beach.

Ana is familiar with this beach now, but if she wasn't, she would find it quite intimidating. The beach is both strikingly beautiful and energetically intense.

You often see only a few people down there, maybe a family or two with their kids and dogs or possibly one of the older, retired couples who live full time in the cove, out taking their daily walk at low tide.

When Ana reached the higher part of the beach, she lost her footing on the slick path and fell fast and hard on her tailbone. Luckily, the jogging stroller didn't get away from her and Lucien remained sound asleep.

The fall wasn't that bad; Ana was just a little hurt. But it felt exceptionally raw.

The fall thrust Ana back into her body. She had been checked out for a long time.

She sat on the rocks and wept, the stroller safe at her side. She was alone with the sleeping baby while Drew was floating around in the ocean just a few miles away. Two different wavelengths. Two different life trajectories. Both experiencing the immense power of the earth.

She felt so much hurt. What she needed was a mother to soothe her and she didn't have one anymore.

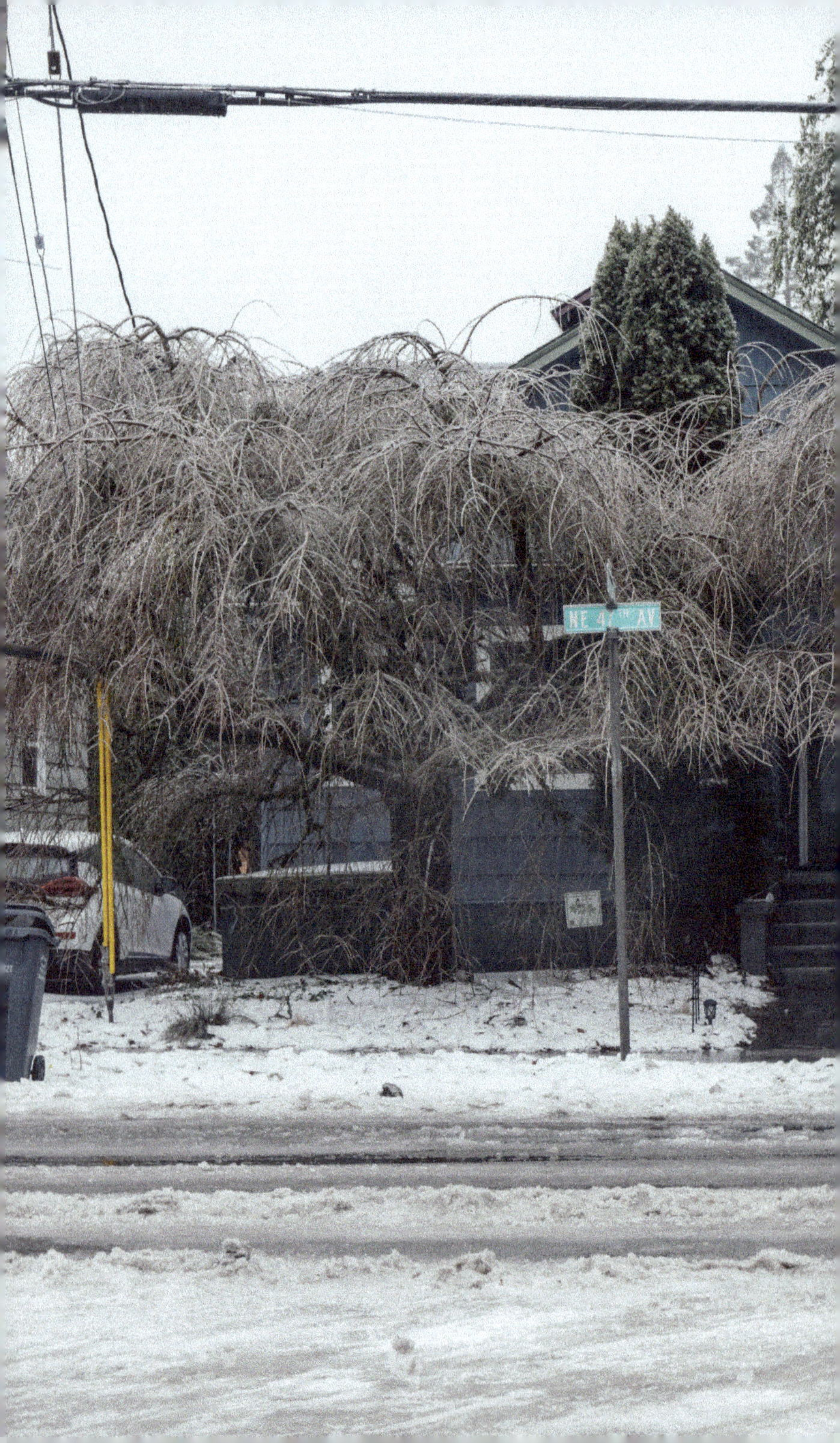
NE 44TH AV

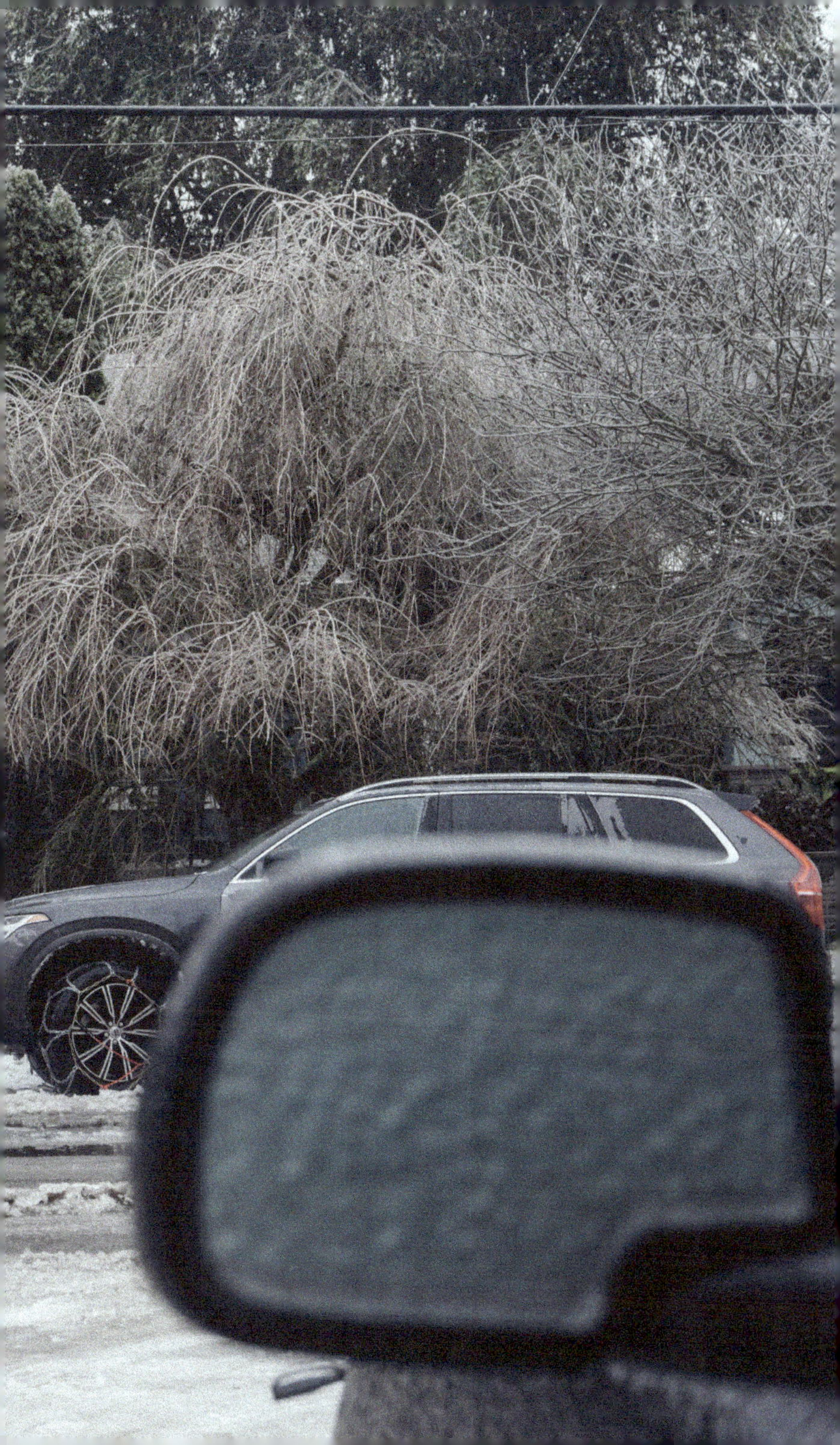

On the Monday morning back home in Portland after a weekend at the coast, Ana experiences a well of appreciation for their comfortable home, the predictability of her morning routine.

She finds subtle joy and a warm satisfaction in preparing breakfast and lunch for Lucien, making a shopping list, and sweeping the floors.

Ana even feels patient with Drew and his avoidance. She looks forward to working on her writing after the child is dropped at school and all the chores are completed.

But Ana knows that the routine will eventually turn back into monotony and that the imbalance with Drew will become evident again. She knows that she will sometimes daydream about having her own home and she will find solace in this fleeting, abstract idea. To not have to witness Drew sleeping peacefully in bed each morning while she makes breakfast, packs lunch for Lucien, feeds the animals, cleans up the kitchen, and reminds the child multiple times to put on socks, to brush his teeth, to get his jacket, his backpack.

It is a certain brand of frustrating to be rushing around the house while your partner is just looking at their phone. Some mornings, the magma builds and then eventually, it recedes. Ana will forget how frustrated she is until the cycle ignites again. And each time she witnesses this pattern, she wonders how someone can just tune out, avoid what is going on around them. The concept of not being seen is such an old wound for Ana, a remnant from childhood that is buried deep inside her body.

These emotions are a convergence being ignored in the present and a history of being neglected: it is a hot red anger.

Where Ana is drawn to the needs around her, Drew turns away from the needs around him. They are often two people moving in opposite directions.

Ana knows that she is not alone She has a friend whose partner does crunches on the living room floor while she struggles frantically to get her two young daughters out of the house in the mornings. Ana has another friend whose spouse tells her he's not a maid when she asks him if he wouldn't mind cleaning up the kitchen.

She finishes the last sip of her morning tea, then goes into the bedroom.

"Can't you at least get yourself up in the morning?" Ana says to Drew.
"Sorry, hon," he says, then rolls out of bed and proceeds to do some yoga stretches in his boxer shorts.
"Drew, you only have like twenty minutes before you guys have to leave."
"Oh shit, okay. I'm coming," he says.

Drew dresses, goes to the bathroom, and starts the kettle. He stands by the counter staring at his phone, first grinding the beans and then preparing a slow, pour-over coffee. Lucien sits at the kitchen table, eating a bowl of organic cereal with thawed blueberries. She gives Lucien chewable multivitamins that he spits out into the toilet, into the garbage can, or under his bed. She makes his lunch, a bagel with cream cheese, and a cut-up apple with cinnamon, both of which will return home either uneaten or hardly eaten.

Every day, Ana makes the lunch and every day, she composts most of it when the child gets home. This has gone on now for about five years.

Ana was the same way as a child. She couldn't eat lunch at

school. She couldn't stand the lunchroom smells, the chaos, the kids eating with their mouths open like little animals. Lucien makes the same complaints that Ana did. But she can't stand the idea of him going hungry, so she just keeps pretending that one day he will eat the lunch.

While Drew eats cereal and sips his coffee at the counter, Ana makes sure that Lucien has everything he needs for school: water bottle, lunch, a signed note so he can go on a walking field trip.

Drew and Lucien leave the house on bikes. Ana sees them ride away and feels a deep sense of relief. She is now left to clean up the breakfast dishes, make the beds, start the laundry, walk the dog. But it's quiet now and that gives her joy.

Ana wonders if it will ever get better, if she needs to leave for it to get better.

The frustration is deep, solid, buried. And then she thinks about putting all of her books into boxes, *you keep this table, I'll take that chair.* She thinks about Lucien being shuttled between two homes. She knows now how traumatizing it was to be uprooted each week, the confusion of two disparate households.

"You'll know if you are ready to leave," Jayne tells Ana one afternoon.
"If I had my own money, I'd probably leave," Ana says.

But Ana doesn't tell Jayne that she knows she will never leave. Ana likes to fantasize about a stark little apartment: a light-filled writing studio, custom floor-to-ceiling bookshelves, a tidy, organized room for Lucien. She likes to think about not having to deal with Drew's messiness anymore.

"I just feel really lonely," Ana tells Jayne.
"I know you do," she softly says to Ana "It's so much worse

living with someone you are not connected to than living alone."

Ana takes no action, makes no changes.

She endures the endless unpaid housework and childcare, all the tedium of micromanaging and facilitating a spouse, a child, two homes, the bills, the groceries, the social calendars. She reads things by strong women who seem to have this shit figured out. These are women with powerful voices. Ana is just another woman trying to make a fuss when she feels that she should just shut the fuck up already.

You don't make money, so you don't have a say. You don't deserve to have a voice and you are deemed powerless.

Ana recognizes how people on the outside see her. *Just be happy in your simple little privileged role with your boutique clothing and your unlimited yoga pass and your cute little writing projects.*

Ana sweeps the kitchen floor and wipes down the bathroom. She starts the dishwasher; she puts a load into the laundry. She makes a list for the grocery store.

And then she leaves on her bike to go to a coffee shop to write for a few hours, because the writing is what gives her meaning in life. That and how much she truly loves her child.

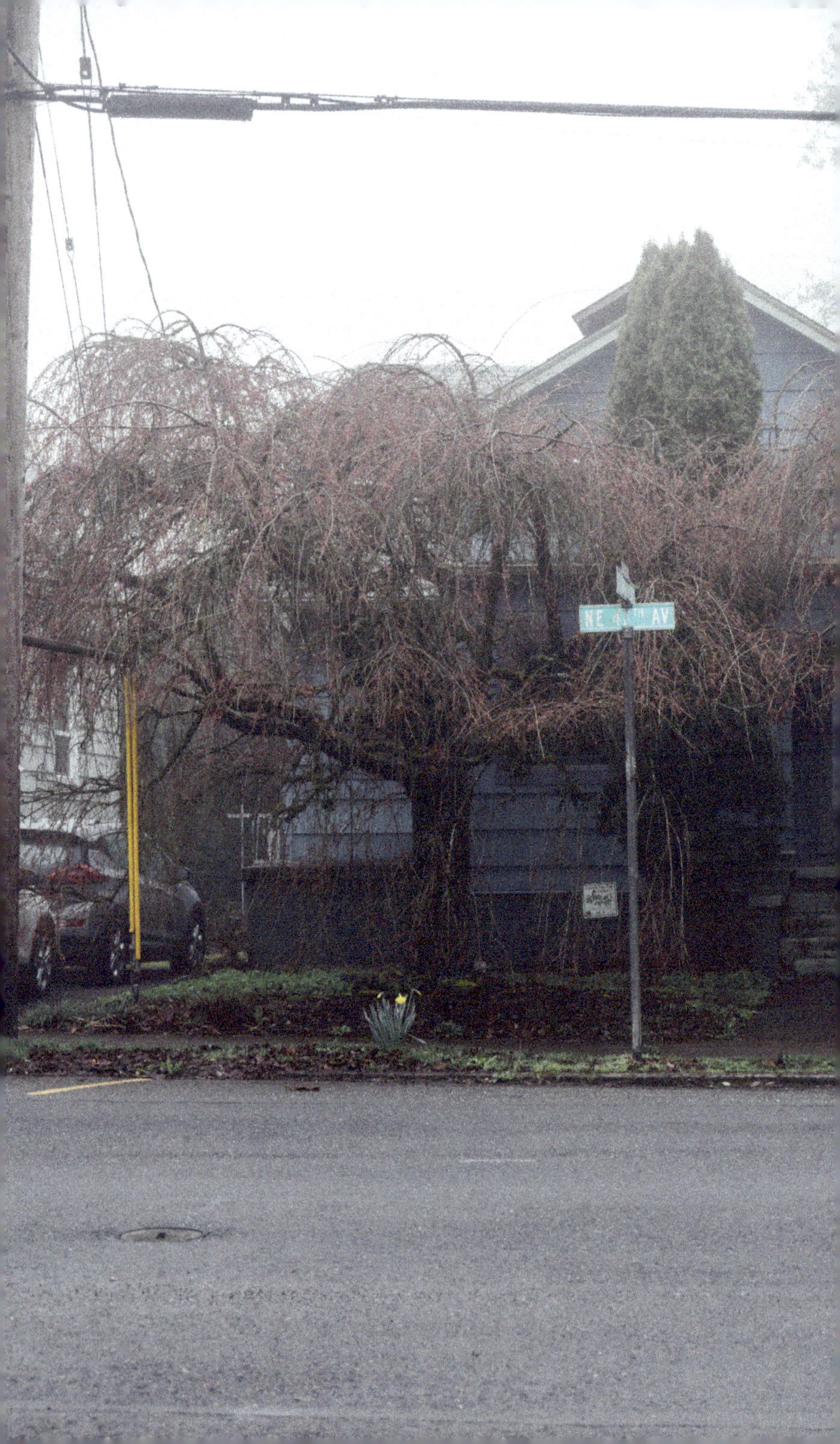

NE 4TH AV

In therapy, Jayne points out to Ana that she has a lot of anxiety. She tells Ana that she didn't feel safe in the world as a kid. She reminds Ana that for years, she turned away from the anxiety. She smoked pot, drank wine, and had lots of thoughtless sex. Now that Ana is facing the traumas head-on, it is as if she is living her way through them all over again and she is finally able to feel all that she couldn't feel as a kid.

Jayne tells Ana that the body doesn't forget—that the trauma stays in our neurological wiring, in our cells, in our nervous systems, until we are ready to heal, if we ever are.

Ana sits quietly and remembers being back at her father's house on a Saturday morning, sitting in her older stepsister's room, afraid to go downstairs because she didn't know what mood her stepmother would be in.

"I feel scared," she tells Jayne.
"Okay, tell me where you feel it."
"In my chest, in my stomach," Ana says. "I'm back at my dad's house."

Ana recalls contacting Jayne out of desperation. She felt like she was no longer tethered to the earth. She would often walk around her neighborhood in a daze, feeling as if she hovered just a few inches above the ground.

She decided to get help. Lucien must have been around five years old at the time.

Ana was finally getting decent sleep and Lucien was in school full time by that point, so she was starting to think clearly for the first time in years.

With that clarity came a tremendous amount of fear and uncertainty, about what, Ana had no idea at the time. Before Lucien, she worked a lot and got fucked up a lot.

Now she doesn't do either.

The change came quick and then it was all about survival mode–learning how to mother a young child. Ana had wanted to have a child with Drew, but she didn't know what it would actually be like to raise a child with him.

When you have a child with someone, she learned in the years after Lucien was born, not only does your relationship change, but your contract with one another is up for negotiation. The contract entails finances, household responsibilities, and child-care duties. All this made Ana realize that Drew is not good at defining roles or negotiating responsibilities.

When she was a kid at her mom's, Ana would be struck with fits of anger. She never understood where the anger came from; she knew it wasn't right, that she needed help. She yelled a lot, threw things, and then felt bad, guilty, broken.

Ana never did anything about the anger and so it never went away.

Lucien was a little over a year old and they had hatched a travel plan over the holidays to take a family trip to Mexico. Portland was covered in a blanket of snow, and Ana was desperate for the healing sun. They went down to Todos Santos, rented a simple bungalow, got some shitty weed and let Lucien run around naked. Drew surfed a bit, but mostly Ana remembers sitting in a hammock in the sun, watching the baby play with a garden hose. She was able to relax for the first time in a long time.

It was the morning after they got back from Mexico and Ana was having a hard time with the shift. Lucien was down for a nap, Drew had left for work, and Ana was thrust back into her reality again.

The weight of taking care of the house and the child, the feelings of isolation and loneliness. Ana was angry that Drew got to leave, while she had to stay.

She stood at the sink, washing dishes and crying hysterically. Then came this anger from the depths. She grabbed Lucien's wooden highchair and threw it against the wall, making a dent in the sheetrock that Ana had to look at for years, until they repainted the kitchen.

She told Drew that the highchair accidentally fell backwards into the wall while she was sweeping. She never had to tell him that she threw the highchair because it didn't break.

This was the second time Ana had dented a wall, and she knew intuitively that the second time was linked to the first.

The first time she was a young kid, angry with her mother for some reason or another, probably something having to do with not paying a utility bill or not having enough money for food. Ana threw a metal aerosol hairspray can at the living room wall, which also made a small dent that she had to look at for years.

The evening sunset casts beautiful glowing orbs on the living room walls. Lucien and Ana are playing with a large pink balloon from a birthday party that the child attended a few days prior. He punches the practically lifeless form towards Ana, and she punches it back.

Drew is in the kitchen frying burgers that Ana smashed together earlier with finely chopped rosemary and diced onion.

While Ana sits on the couch, punching the balloon to her son, she realizes that she feels like a much older person, more like those worn-out grandparents that she sees struggling to chase their grandkids at the park. She can feel the drooping of her eyes, the aching in her lower back and a pain radiating from her pelvis.

She's tried hard to get to the bottom of this pain. She has seen a variety of practitioners and taken herbal remedies and pharmaceutical medications. It will seem like something is working, but then after some time, she will have another flare up. So Ana has learned to live with it, to ride the pain waves, to salve them however and whenever she can.

Jayne has told her that it probably has something to do with the tension of her early life. How she never felt safe in the world, and that translated to not feeling safe in her body.

After some time, Drew calls Ana and Lucien to dinner. They sit at the kitchen table, and they eat their burgers, the dog lurking at their feet, pining for scraps.

> "I'll stay and clean up," Ana tells Drew when they are done eating. "How about you guys take the dog to the park?"
> "Uh, okay," Drew says, staring at his phone and avoiding eye contact.

Ana notices that Drew tends to bristle when she asks him to do something. She believes that it is a residual effect of being raised by a strict father who would force him to do chores. Drew has mentioned on multiple occasions how he would be yanked out of bed super early on weekend mornings to mow the lawn.

So now Drew doesn't like to be told what to do, even though Ana is more asking than telling. But she senses that he sees it as telling.

Ana had done the grocery shopping earlier that day, prepped the dinner, washed and folded laundry. She's been home with Lucien since he got home from school, made him a snack, helped him with homework.

She just needs a short break from the householding and the care-giving. And she is desperate for the time and space to do something to soothe her pain. But if Ana stated these actual needs to Drew, telling him that she wasn't feeling well and needed some time alone, Drew's avoidance would only hurt more.

He will take Lucien and the dog to the park, of course he will. But he won't be able to empathize with Ana's pain, so oftentimes, she doesn't bother saying what she is really feeling or needing.

Once they put on their hats and jackets and collect the dog, Drew and Lucien leave the house to go to the park. Ana sits at the kitchen table drinking water, staring out the window, waving as they walk by.

She gets up and clears the table, puts remaining food scraps into the compost bin and loads the dishwasher. She lights a chunk of incense and brings it room to room to clear the air. She takes a hot shower and follows it with a cold rinse, because that often helps ease the pain. And then she puts on flannel pajamas and crawls into bed with a heavy library book and a hot water bottle on her abdomen.

When she thinks too much about the pain, she fills with dread about a future living in constant discomfort even though she knows that it tends to ebb and flow. As much as a break is most likely coming, it's hard to believe when she's in the valley of it.

Drew and Lucien don't know how much and how often Ana suffers, because she doesn't talk to them about it. She doesn't want to worry Lucien with her troubles and Drew would just peer at her with glazed-over eyes which would make her feel worse.

After some time, Ana hears them come back into the house, so she calls out to Lucien that he needs to shower and brush his teeth and then he can watch a few shows next to her in bed. When she doesn't hear the shower, Ana yells to Drew.

"Okay," Drew says, after a pause.

Ana senses his tone, as if she is interrupting something important, even though she knows that he is on Instagram looking at photos of happy people living their super epic lives.

"Hey," she says, once she hears the shower running.
"Yeah, hon," Drew says, after a long pause.
"I don't feel great, so I'm gonna stay in bed," Ana says.

Drew doesn't say anything back. Ana lays in bed with her knees pulled up to her chest and weeps silently, out of pain and loneliness.

"You need to tell him, so he at least knows, but you can't expect anything back," Jayne had told Ana recently.
"That's so hard," she said.
"Yes, it is," Jayne said.

Lucien gets out of the shower, puts on his pajamas, and curls up next to Ana.

Ana can tell that the child knows that she is hurting, because she knows that Lucien has an awareness his father does not have. There is a lot he has learned from her. He kisses Ana on the cheek.

And then she reads while the boy watches an episode or two. Every few minutes, Lucien makes his mother put her book down so she can watch a crucial scene.

Ana realizes that she is not in as much pain anymore. Jayne often tells her that two things heal physical pain: one is love and the other is rest.

The next morning the bedroom is filled with a deep blue light.

Ana forces herself out of bed, while Drew stirs and smacks his lips in his sleep. The dog hears Ana rustling about, comes into the bedroom and sidles up to her side of the bed, his eyes alert, anticipating his morning treats.

Ana dresses in a few warm layers and goes into the kitchen. She puts on the kettle and gives the dog his treats before letting him out and giving him his breakfast.

She prepares herself a cup of milky black tea and then takes to her chair in the living room. The morning while her family is still in bed is her favorite time of the day. Ana sits for a few moments in meditation and then opens her notebook, grabs a pen, and stares at a blank page for a while.

She sips some tea and ends up texting with a friend back in New York. A way to connect when she is feeling lonely. They've gotten a snowstorm back east and Ana writes to tell her friend how she wishes she could be there to see the city covered in a deep blanket of fresh snow.

> *There's nothing like it in the world,* Ana writes.
> *Until it turns to dirty slush,* her friend responds
> *Ha, you're right!* Ana writes.

Ana drinks her tea and reminisces about the snowstorms of her East Coast youth and young adulthood. She has always enjoyed looking out the window and watching the snow fall. It's one of her favorite things in life.

A snowstorm often meant a day or two off school and even though her home life was never great, she did appreciate the break in routine, away from the blaring television that was the soundtrack to her youth. And the connection back to the seasons. She could always find friends to trudge around in the snow with. She loved the feeling of bundling up and heading out into the white abyss.

With the last of her tea now finished, Ana knows that it is time to wake up the child and get him ready for school. Her work day as a mother begins, another winter day.

The light in the living room has turned a flat gray.

> "Come say hi to Mom when you're dressed," Ana says loudly so Lucien can hear her from his bedroom, down the short hallway from the living room.

Lucien bounds over moments later, eyes still sleepy and flops onto the couch. Ana walks over, covers him with a blanket and gives him a big kiss on his head.

Ana makes Lucien two organic flax toaster waffles piled with frozen blueberries that she thawed in warm water, and then adds yogurt, cinnamon, and maple syrup.

Ana feels like she should make more wholesome homemade food, not these cardboard frozen pucks. The child eats and reads comics while Ana prepares a smoothie and two fried eggs for herself. When Lucien is done eating, he runs off to his room while Ana eats at the counter and puts together his lunch.

Drew doesn't say a word to Ana when he comes into the kitchen. She leaves him a little bit of smoothie in the blender, which he pours into a small glass cup. He sits at the kitchen table, drinks the smoothie, and munches loudly on a bowl of cereal. Ana feels her skin crawling at the sound of the spoon hitting the bottom of the bowl, the gnashing of the cereal between Drew's teeth.

Ana goes into Lucien's room and gives the boy two jackets to choose from. They walk back into the kitchen together, where

Drew is grinding his coffee.

"It's raining so I guess I'll drive Lucien to school," Ana says. "Oh okay, cool," he says, clearly not aware of the time.

Ana puts on her coat, gets the car keys, and wrangles the child off to school.

Drew and Ana are in the kitchen making dinner when Ana brings up plans for Lucien's spring break which is in a few weeks. They are planning to spend some time at their cabin on the coast with another family, close friends who also have a son around Lucien's age.

While chopping kale at the counter, Ana asks Drew if he could please not leave her at the house with the other mom the whole time. Don't just assume it's okay to leave them to watch the kids while he and the other dad go out surfing.

> "I just want there to be more of a balance this time," Ana says, calmly. "Last time I was really burned out by the time we left to come home."

Drew won't look at her even though she is standing right beside him. She can feel the energy shift in the kitchen. She can almost hear his inner voice telling himself that he is the one who makes the money, that Ana should have nothing to complain about.

Ana would like to explain how she often feels so trapped and frustrated when they are at the beach. How it saddens her that she used to enjoy going out there to hike and surf and smoke pot and sit in the sun with a book. Now being at the coast just escalates the typical frustration and anger that she experiences at home.

She knows that things are different now; she knows that she is different now.

> "All I am asking is for you to be more aware when you think about going surfing for hours," she says.
> "Can't you just sit in the house and read?" Drew fires back.
> "Not with kids who need things," Ana says, her voice rising. "I swear, you're just another one of those dickhead assholes!"

Later that evening, after the kitchen is cleaned up from dinner and Lucien is in his bedroom playing video games, Ana tries to talk to Drew again. She is concerned that the child can hear them, but she continues.

She knows that Drew wants to flee the scene. But he stays seated at the kitchen table, nervously folding a cloth napkin around his iPhone, as if he is swaddling a baby, his precious phone baby.

"This time here together is limited," Ana says. "I just want you to know, so you are aware of how I really feel."

Ana looks directly at Drew. She feels strong. Drew looks back at her, his eyes turning red but there are no tears.

"There might be someone out there who can actually care about me," Ana says.

"But I care for you," Drew says.

"You only think that you do, but it's all about you in the end."

"It's not, hon..."

"When I bring something up, you immediately get defensive."

"I know," Drew says. "I feel attacked."

"I am just trying to talk to you," Ana says.

When the words come out of her mouth, it feels wrong, like she is doing this awful thing by confronting Drew. She knows why he's like this, even though he doesn't. Ana knows that it is not her role in life to tell him that he needs fixing. He would need to figure this out for himself.

"It's like you are on your own private boat, paddling along next to me," Ana says, picturing the two of them rowing separate boats side by side, his moving farther ahead and hers constantly lagging behind.

"I want to be on the same boat," she says. "I want to be rowing together. What if my boat gets a hole in it and sinks?"

"I would save you," he says.

Ana wants nothing more than to believe that Drew would save her, but she doesn't think he would. She doesn't think he has it in him to protect her.

He wants to, he really does—he just doesn't know how.

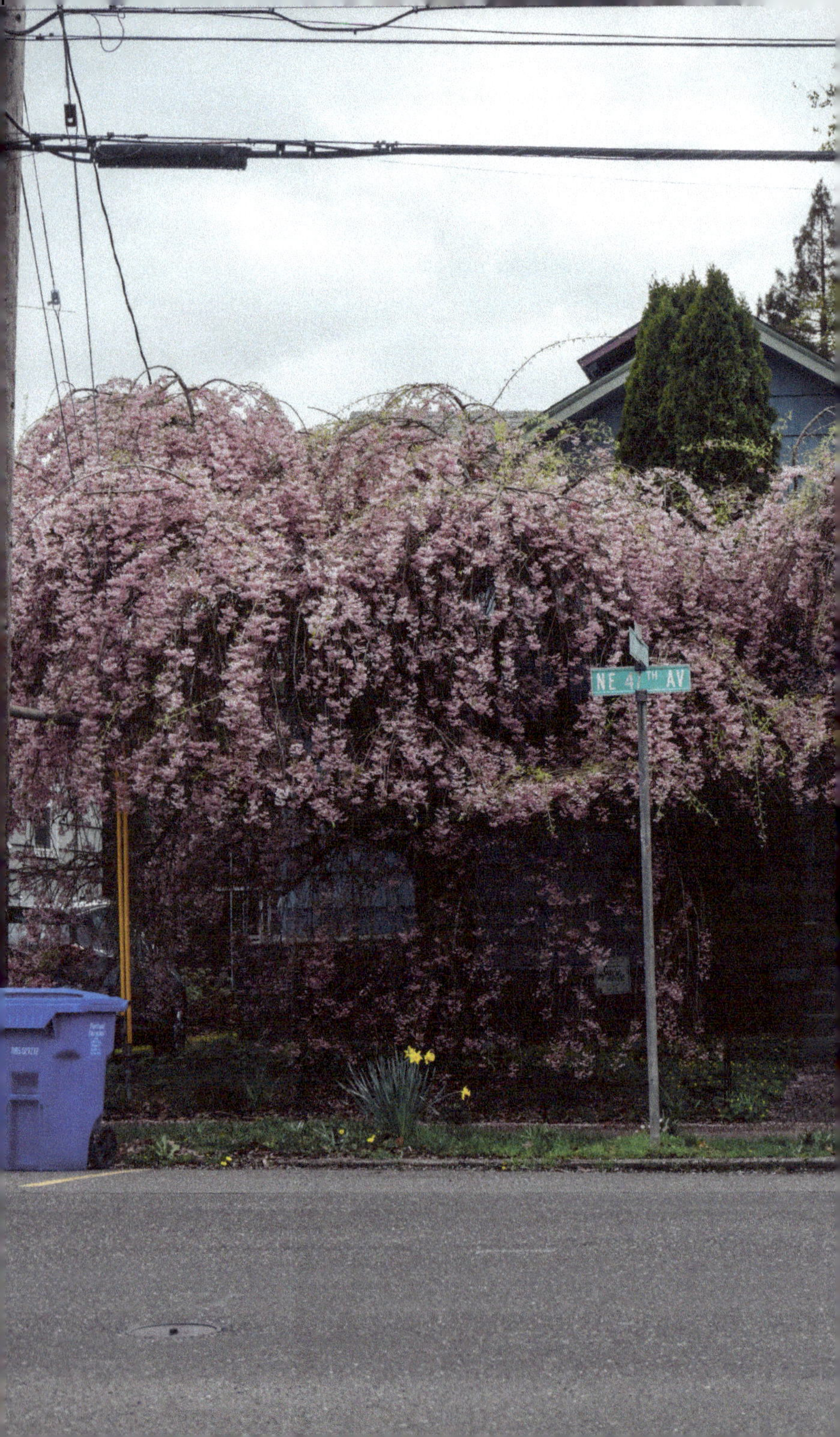
NE 47TH AV

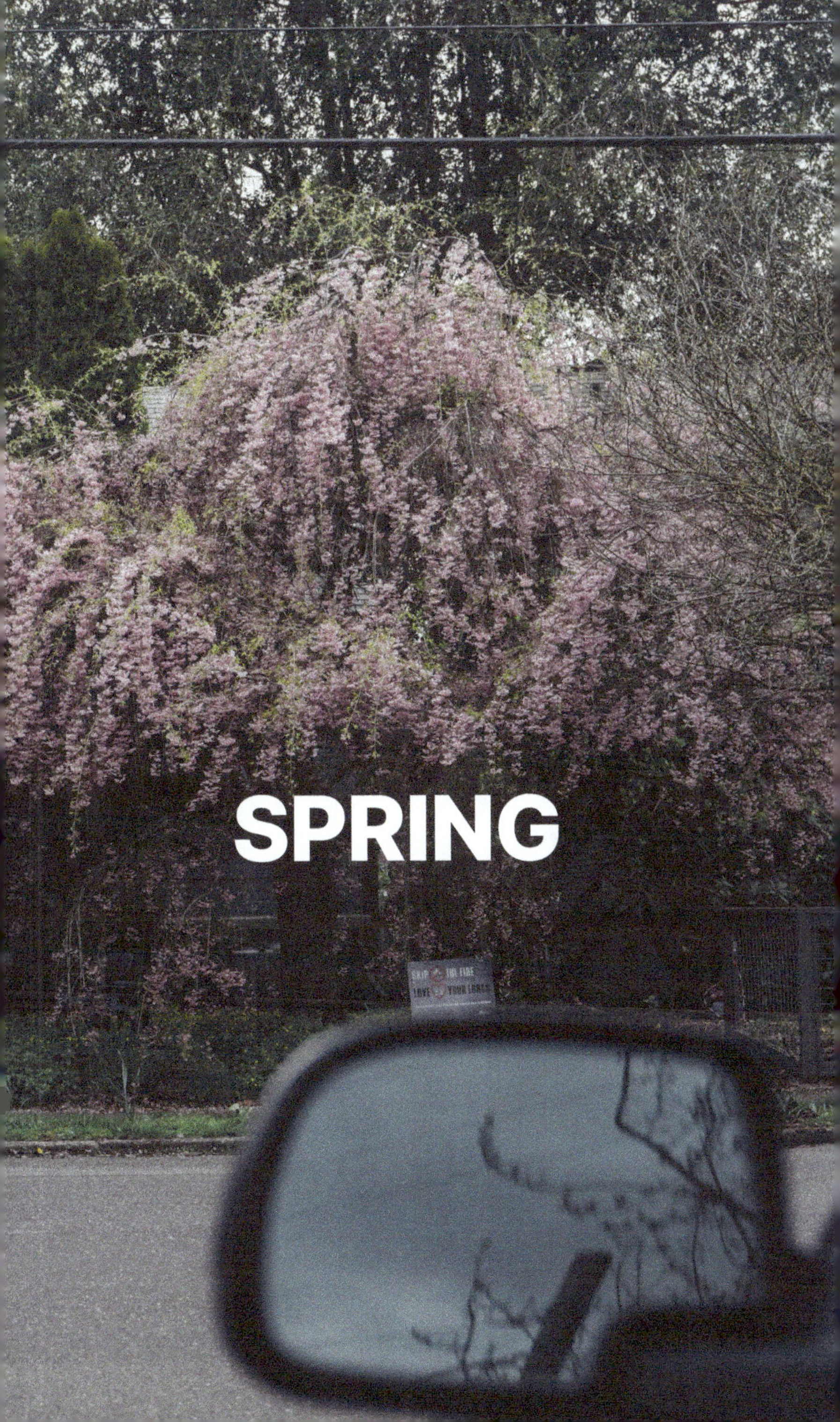
SPRING

It feels like it will never stop raining.

When the sun does come out, it's fleeting. Things this year feel different—this spring. Everyone seems to be complaining about how wet it has been, but Ana doesn't mind. She figures it might mean that they won't have so many wildfires this summer, and less days of extreme heat.

Some mornings, she wakes up feeling like someone has inserted their hands inside her chest, strangling her heart, pressing down on her lungs, not letting go.

It's like being choked from inside of her body, she thinks.

> "Oh, I get that too—that's dread," a friend said over lunch recently.
> "You're right. It's existential dread!" Ana responded.
> "But I get mine in my stomach, not my chest," her friend said.

Even now, so many years later—Ana can recall the exact sensation of childhood dread and how it felt like someone sneaking up and stealing her breath away. She has always been sensitive and extra aware of her surroundings.

She can recall sleeping in her father's house in Jersey, this was during the brief period when they still lived in his house as a complete family—before her parents' divorce, and remembers how, many nights, she would wake up in terror.

Once, her parents carried her from bed, down the

stairs, through the kitchen and into the laundry room in the middle of the night, probably so she wouldn't wake the rest of the house with her cries. Ana remembers her parents sitting her on top of the washing machine and talking to her calmly. This is one of the only memories of her parents together in an intimate moment, side by side, caring for their youngest child.

A few years after that incident, her mother moved out after the divorce and only a few more years later, her stepmother, who was prone to horrific bouts of rage, moved in along with her three adult children. They were strangers, and it was as if her mother and her older siblings had been replaced by this new cast of characters.

It didn't feel safe, because they weren't safe people. They were all adults and she was a young child who couldn't protect herself and her father could not always protect her because he had to tend to the needs of his new wife.

For many years after this, it seemed the dread was gone. But she now understands that the dread was just buried but definitely not gone.

Even though she is nourished by her relationships, there are times when engaging socially feels like too much for Ana.

She can sense when she is burning out and needs to be alone, quiet for a while. There are days when having Drew around feels like too much. Lucien's presence generally provides joy and comfort for Ana. Caring for him can be very soothing, something that she can lean on as a salve for her nervous system. That is, unless he is having a teen meltdown.

When Lucien was much younger and would have epic tantrums, her emotions would flood. The loudness and chaos of the toddler would send her spiraling, dredging up buried memories and propelling her into a detached, dissociative state.

It saddens her to recall a time she forcefully placed the boy on his bed and shut the door to his bedroom, leaving him alone to scream and thrash about. Ana knows that Drew was often present during these tantrums, but she doesn't remember how involved he got, if at all.

It took Ana years to recognize that the child's emotional chaos brought her old traumas to the surface, but Ana can now see that she did the best that she could.

There are lots of times that Ana feels like Drew takes too much from her. That he doesn't know how to give anything back. Ana has come to believe this is because he wasn't provided with a certain level of care as a child. She knows that there are times in their partnership that she is a replacement mother. Even though Drew may never admit to it, she can feel it through his needs and actions. And she knows that she has played into it for the past twenty-something years of their relationship, enabling him to be dependent on her for stupid things like making shopping lists or ensuring that he goes to the doctor.

Ana often reminds Drew multiple times to do things, not unlike her teen son.

She is aware of Drew's helplessness. She used to get angry and frustrated with him, which would push him further away. Once she realized why he was like that and that he had no path to changing these behaviors (even though she practically begged him to) she became more accepting and often finds it easier to just do whatever the task is, instead of having to ask Drew to do it over and over again.

This is because Ana has made the choice to look at her own actions and behaviors, which in turn has made Drew's actions and behaviors more about him and less about her.

Sometimes, though, she just cannot be around another nervous system, especially one that has been wounded and neglected like his.

These days, Ana usually wakes in the morning with a chest full of anxiety. She has no choice but to proceed with her day and little by little, the sensations of dread become easier to manage.

Her priority each day is to make sure that Lucien has what he needs, that he eats well, that his emotional needs are being met, that he gets off to school okay. She takes the dog for a long walk and makes herself breakfast. She always does what needs to be done around the house. On the days when she feels calm enough to sit quietly, she will meditate and practice yoga.

Only then can Ana tend to her writing: this is her work. It is what brings her the most fulfillment and joy outside of mothering Lucien.

In the afternoon, if the anxiety comes in and if it's too strong, she calls someone, someone whose voice and conversation will ground her. Maybe her brother or her good friend back in Jersey.

Then once the sun goes down, she is mostly okay again. Ana wonders if this pattern has something to do with the rhythm of her childhood and teen years.

> In the mornings, Ana had to wake up and face either her mother or her stepmother. Her mother

could be feigning illness on the pullout couch in the living room, a moaning pile in a mess of unwashed sheets and blankets. Her stepmother could be frantically cleaning the house, running the vacuum cleaner like a tyrant, yelling to her father that the house was always so dirty, that nobody ever helped her.

And then on school days, she would return alone to the apartment she shared with her mother, a classic 80s era latchkey kid. Ana was always scared to be alone, constantly worrying that someone would break in and attack her or that a ghost would jump out of a closet.

When her mother would come panting up the stairs in the evenings—even though she wasn't the most stable person—Ana would at least feel somewhat safe again. Her mother would rustle up dinner and then she and Ana would sit together in the living room watching sitcoms until it was time to go to bed.

Ana now looks forward to the time after dinner, when the kitchen is put back together and everyone's needs are met.

She has also developed an inherent need for order, another side effect being raised in chaos. If something is out of place, she must fix it right away. When she sees something that isn't right, her heart beats faster. If a closet door is open, she has to get up to shut it. If there is a pile of dishes in the sink, she needs to put them in the dishwasher. If the bathroom is dirty, she wipes it down.

Recently, Ana was on the phone with her brother, and they were talking about their mother. She was on a dog walk and he was at home in Jersey. They were laughing about how their mother was something of a minor crook back in the day, how she would often bounce checks or go into arrears on utility bills and rent.

Ana got another call from her brother a few hours later, but he wasn't laughing anymore. His tone was different, solemn. He was no longer joking around.

"Mom was different before the divorce," he said.
"What do you mean?" Ana asked him.
"When she was with Dad, she wasn't like that," he told Ana.

Unlike Ana, her brother has memories of a stable mother. Longer days now, and evening is dappled with light and the scent of warm rain and grass.

Ana takes a hot shower, rubs a few drops of lavender essential oil onto her neck and chest, puts on a soft pair of cotton pajamas. She settles on the couch with a wool blanket, reads for a bit, then looks for something to watch on her laptop.

Lucien and Drew are doing their own things, in their own spaces.

Sometimes Lucien will come sit with Ana on the couch and she will experience a similar sense of comfort that she would feel when she would sit in the living room with her mother and the TV. They'll watch a few episodes, the boy leaning his head on her shoulder.

And then he'll go back upstairs to be a teenager.

The cat appears and crawls onto her lap. She scratches the cat behind her ears, kisses her on her nose. The cat will soon be three years old.

It was spring, around this time of year, when a friend's cat had a litter of kittens.

Ana and Lucien helped care for the kittens because the friend and her family were out of town a lot. They were promised a kitten once they were ready to leave the mother cat. Lucien, who was eleven at the time, was thrilled. He had been asking for a cat for a long time.

Ana's friend's home is a gorgeous two-story farmhouse on an oversized lot in North Portland. She is a master gardener with impeccable, simple taste and it felt healing to be in her lovely home with those adorable kittens.

Even so, Ana was struggling so much.

There were six kittens in the litter. Lucien researched how to figure out their sexes and created a handwritten spreadsheet of sorts. He chose the one female kitten to take home, a matte gray who eventually morphed into a gray tabby.

They named her Saskia. The name came to Ana, she said it aloud, and the child loved it.

Over the course of about a month, they watched the kittens go from a small cardboard box to a larger cardboard box to a gated pen to their own room. Sometimes Lucien would bring a friend with them. Ana found it really sweet watching these awkward preteens dote on the tiny kittens. They loved watching them nurse on the mother, a mysterious black cat named Kiki who would come and go throughout the day. Once the kittens started running amok through the house, Ana's friend doled them out to separate homes.

It was such a precious time, an exceptionally hard time.

"It's an anniversary time," Jayne said to Ana last spring.
"What do you mean an anniversary time?" Ana asked.
"Oh, it's just that our bodies can remember echoes of hard times until we are fully healed," she told Ana.

A few years prior during springtime, Ana had published a story about a young woman whose mother dies just a few months before she was to become a mother herself.

Ana had written the story to make sense of her own grief.

She happened to be with Drew and Lucien in Manhattan on the day the piece ran in an online literary journal. They were staying at an Airbnb in Chelsea. A good friend of Ana's was getting married upstate, so they flew back east and spent some time in the city beforehand.

Ana got up early, well before Drew and Lucien were awake, and left the apartment to go to a coffee shop around the corner. Seeing her published story online made Ana feel kind of how she felt on her birthday, but different, even better.

She sat at a small marble bistro table near the expansive front windows sipping strong coffee. The bright morning sun cast a glow onto the old wooden windowsills. Ana read, sketched out some ideas in her journal, and observed the comings and goings of the urban morning.

Sometimes she would pull out her phone and look back at her published story. A few people sat nearby in the front area, while other folks bustled in and out, grabbing a quick coffee before heading into work. She remembered being one of them. It had been almost twenty years since she took the PATH train from Jersey City to an ad agency in the Flatiron District, always stopping off for a cheap deli coffee before starting her work day.

Sitting at that cafe, she was finally able to bask in something joyful. Just as it was to bring Lucien into the world during the grief of losing her mother, sharing this story was also a complex joy, tremendously difficult but also filled with love.

87

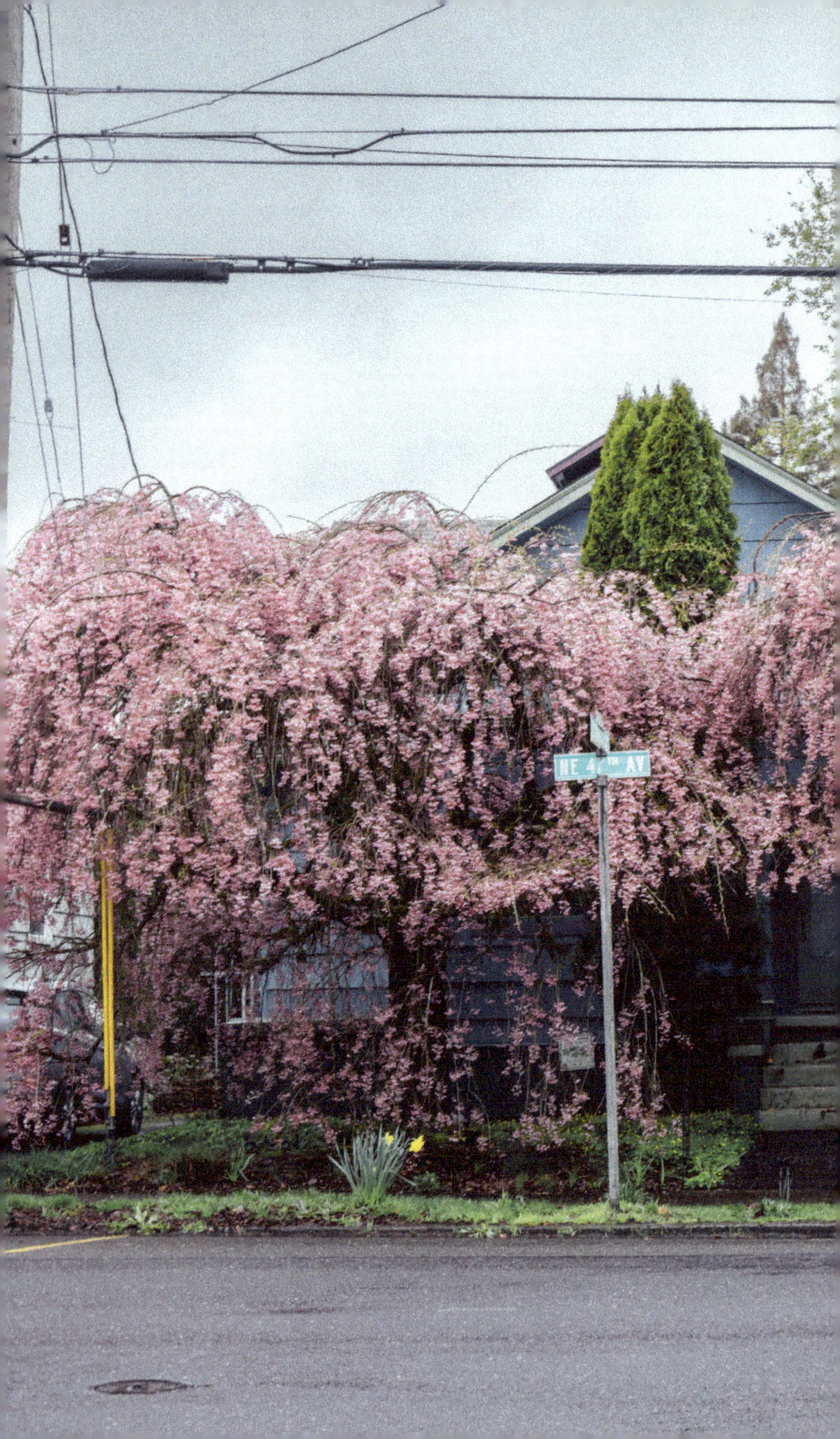
NE 4?TH AV

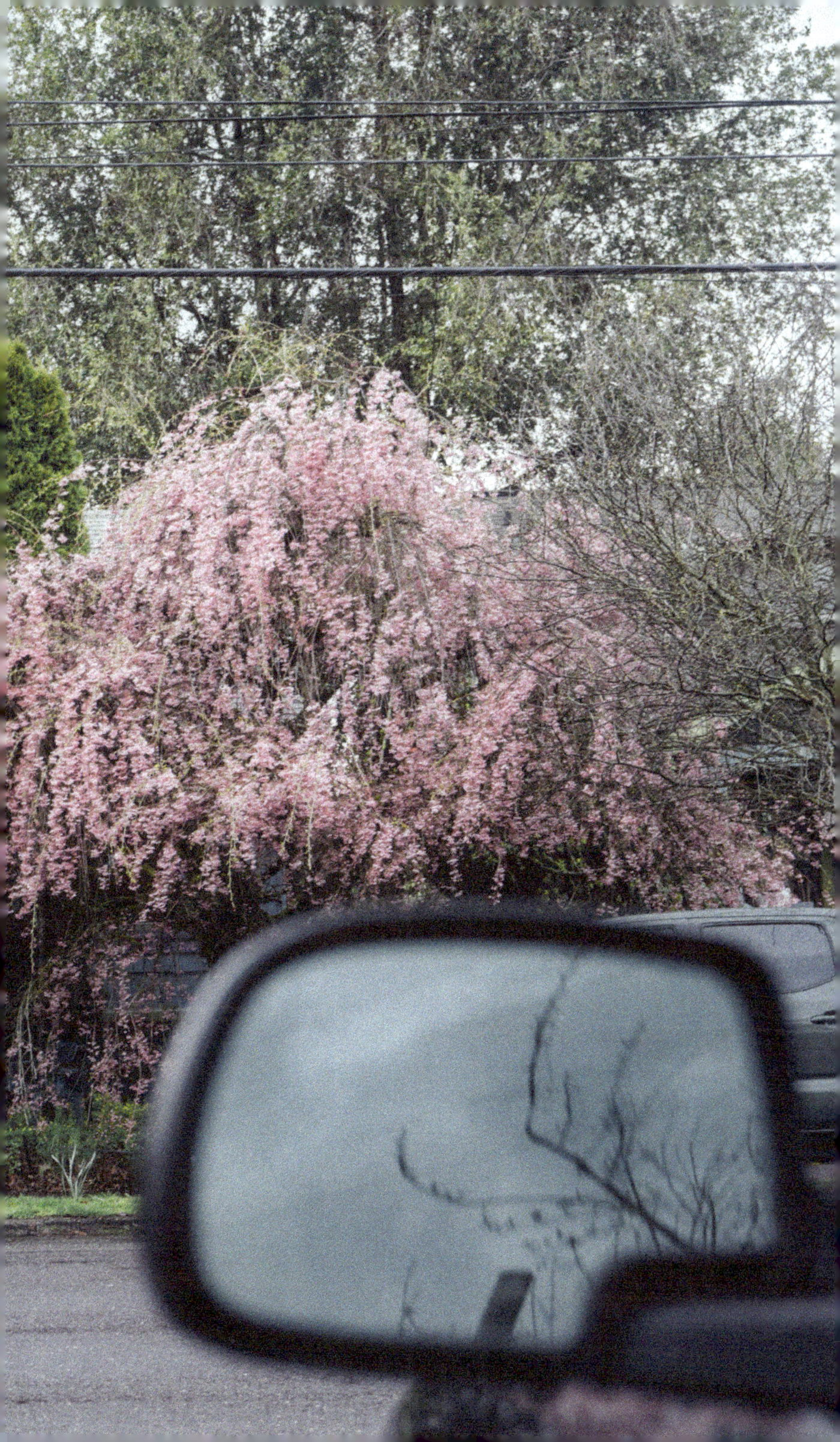

When Ana returned home to Portland, she felt as if someone had flipped a switch, causing her nervous system to short circuit. Something felt terribly wrong, though she couldn't name what. Ana remained in that state through the end of spring, throughout most of the summer and well into fall. She was barely able to function during the day, and hardly able to sleep at night.

Drew would bring Ana herbal tea and granola with yogurt and fruit, that she would take in bed as if she was infirm. There were a few days that she even asked Drew to work from home, just so she didn't have to be alone.

"I've never seen anyone get like this," he said to Ana one morning, as she lay on Drew, weeping.

Drew was very kind to Ana during that time. She doesn't think he truly understood what was going on with her and she had to specifically state her needs, but at least he could be there for her.

At first, Ana had a hard time trusting Drew because she felt like he turned away from her when Lucien was a baby, when she was so sleep-deprived and shelled. But she also doesn't think she was very nice to him then, because she was so angry with grief.

A friend of his had dealt with anxiety before, so he was somewhat familiar with it. The friend often complained of a pain in his left arm, would think that he was having a heart attack and would go to the ER only to find out that nothing was physically wrong. It was so much easier to recognize anxiety in someone else.

Jayne would tell her over and over that this anxiety was inside of her all along but had been lying dormant for many years.

"This is how you must have felt as a young child," Jayne told Ana.

"But I don't get why I am feeling it now," Ana would say.

"You get it when you can handle it—when you are ready to feel it."

It took Ana a long time to fully comprehend what Jayne was saying to her during the panic times. Jayne would share these insights with her, and she could somewhat absorb them, but it would take a long time for them to truly integrate.

"You were floating down a river and you got caught in an eddy," Ana's doctor said to her one afternoon as she was lying on a treatment table, her body covered with acupuncture needles. "I think you are holding in a lot of grief," she said, "You just need to cry."

And so Ana wept years and years of grief and fear, as if a faucet had been opened.

During the months Ana was stuck in the eddy, she saw a multitude of alternative healthcare practitioners: naturopathic medicine, Chinese medicine, craniosacral therapy, functional medicine, chiropractic adjustments, shiatsu massage. And then there were all the sessions with Jayne.

Because Ana wasn't working, she cashed out a modest inheritance that she received when her father passed away a few years prior. She looked at it as a disability payment of sorts that would cover all of this overly expensive, ridiculously privileged care. Ana figured that it was partly her father's fault that she was so fucked up anyhow.

He was a great person, but maybe not an ideal parent. He turned away from Ana as a kid; he allowed her stepmother to treat her horribly and didn't save her from her mother's neglectful patterns.

There was no way that she could have worked in that debilitating state. It would take Ana many months to even attempt to start writing again.

During the deep anxiety times, Ana thought that she would be stuck forever. That's the thing with anxiety, it plays tricks on you, making you think that things aren't okay even though they are. It hooks you into believing the fears are real. When you feel that heightened level of fear, you can't imagine that there will be a time that you won't feel it anymore.

Even though she had support and care, nobody could pull her out of the eddy. She had to find a way out on her own.

Before this, Ana had been working at a liberal arts college, doing editorial work and project management. It was a job that seemed great on the surface: beautiful college campus, great amenities, stellar benefits. But on the inside, it was a toxic work environment where the women did most of the hard laboring while the men stood around busting each other's balls.

She had worked there for about a year when she decided she had to leave.

Ana came to the job with a lot of experience, mostly in terms of project management skills—she had worked in the advertising industry for over a decade. That was her career before Lucien. Her editorial skills were mostly intuitive and untrained, but solid, and she was learning.

But she didn't feel like she was seen for her strengths, nor did she feel respected.

More than anything, she couldn't ignore the mirror—the exact problems we face in our society: power differentials, misogyny, and deep-rooted issues that are often veiled by a progressive, liberal label—enacted at the institution, one she was part of.

Ana knew that this job was not in alignment. So, around the time that her grief story was about to be published, she was also in the process of leaving a job that offered a lot of stability and security.

This is when Ana came apart.

It was a glorious, sunny, spring day and Ana had walked from campus to a local cafe where she would often go for lunch. She ate stir-fry and drank a kombucha on the roof deck. After lunch, she had a scheduled exit meeting with human resources.

Ana walked back to campus, put her bag away at her desk and went upstairs to the HR department.

The college's administration building is quite old and just what you would imagine for a classic American liberal arts college. The old building smell, the sounds of footsteps on the polished concrete floors.

While Ana was sitting with the HR manager, she slipped into a state of panic. She doesn't consider it a panic attack in the classic sense because she didn't pull out of it for a long time; true panic attacks are much shorter—your nervous system can only fuel them that way for so long.

Ana and the HR manager were sitting side by side at her desk, two large windows at their backs, both staring into a computer screen, going over options for insurance severance. Ana wouldn't say that this HR person was nice, and she wouldn't say she was mean. She seemed neutral. Overcome with panic, Ana just sat there and muscled through the meeting, doing her best to hold it together.

She was losing health insurance and a salary. She hadn't made any money since Lucien was born, so Ana had really thought this job was going to be the answer to so many of their financial woes.

"It's the golden handcuffs," a friend who used to work at the college with her said after leaving.

This was a pattern when it came to full-time office jobs. She can count at least three times that she bailed after about a year. Something about doing the same thing day after day. So she would leave, back into uncertainty and instability, a state she knew well.

When Ana finished her meeting with the HR manager, she went

back downstairs for a department meeting. She was still feeling quite panicky. Ana and four coworkers sat around a small table in her supervisor's office.

And then the panic got worse.

She told her coworkers that she felt like she was going to throw up, that something was wrong with her stomach. Ana's coworkers looked at her with wide eyes. She quickly closed her laptop, grabbed a few things at her desk and left the building.

It is a spectacular, leafy campus and it was always a strange feeling walking down the pathways not being a student, not being a professor.

She had gone to a state school in New Jersey for undergrad. Ana was not liberal arts college material. Had she given half a shit about grades in high school, had her parents given half a shit about her in high school, had they come from a different educational or socioeconomic class—maybe she could have been liberal arts college material.

Ana was certainly a bright, creative kid—she just had no guidance, no direction, no support. There was no cool art or English teacher that took her aside to say that she could really be something, someday—that she should work on her grades and apply to this or that program.

Most of her teachers just shook their heads at her when she underperformed.

Spending her days on such a beautiful campus often felt disorienting. Ana would look at the students and think so many things to herself: *they must have good parents who care. They must come from money.* It was obvious that they were smart kids, as it was a highly competitive school and so she often felt lesser than around them even though she was so much older, had so much more life experience. A few of the colleagues in Ana's department were alumni and there was something about them that seemed superior. Maybe it just seemed that way to her.

The walk to her car would have taken about ten minutes. She knows that she must have been shaking, walking fast, trying not to make eye contact with anyone. She remembers the sun was blaring.

Her heart was racing, and it felt like it was going to explode, which made the panic still worse. She wondered if she might be having a heart attack. She shouldn't have driven, but she also didn't feel comfortable telling anyone what was really going on.

Ana would soon learn how to ask for help.

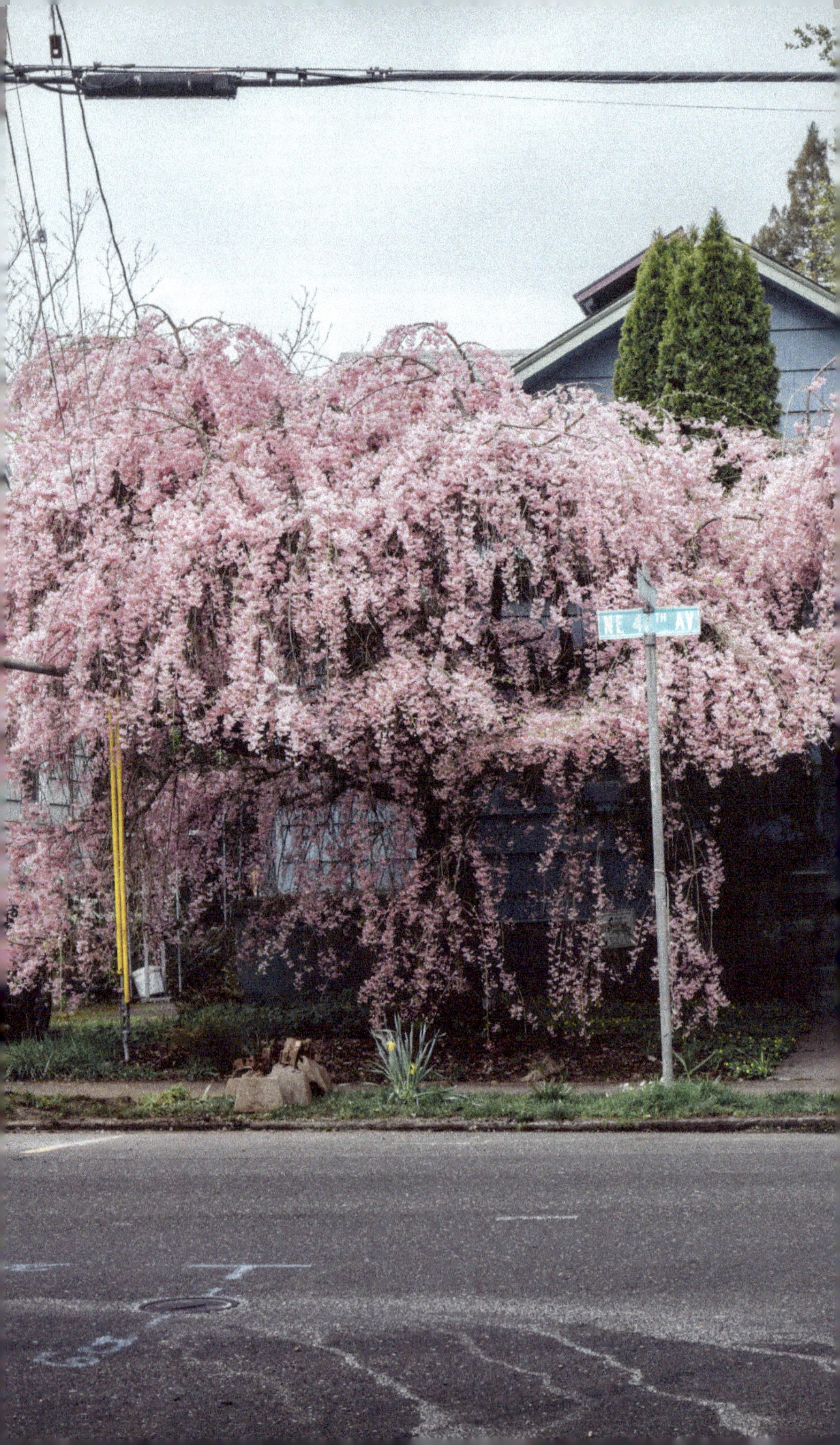
NE 46TH AV

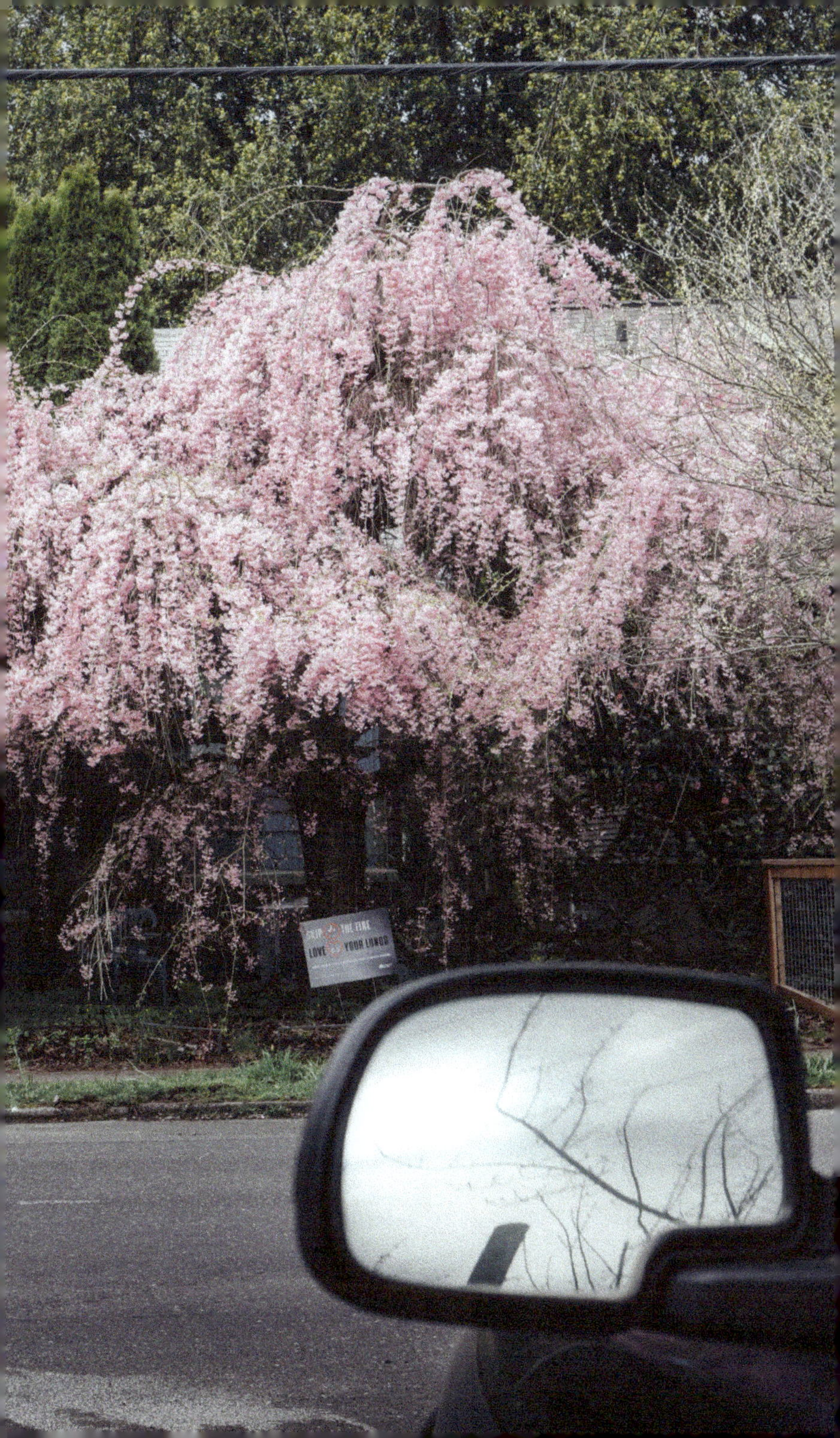
THE FIRE
LOVE YOUR LUNGS

When Ana got home, Drew was working in his studio in the attic. She went upstairs and collapsed on the guest bed across the room.

"I'm not feeling right. I'm feeling panicked," she told him.
"Oh no. That sucks, hon," he said.
"I can't do it," Ana told him, "I just can't do it."
"You can't do what?" he asked.
"The reading...I can't do it."

She was referring to a literary event that was happening later that week. A band would play, and writers would read their work. The event would be held at a local pub not far from their house, a casual venue with old furniture and tons of books scattered about.

She wondered if this could be the reason for her panic. She had participated in a few readings before, but this one felt different. She had been planning to read her recently published story–her most personal, vulnerable work yet.

"It was a perfect storm," Jayne said to Ana.
"I still don't get it," she responded.
"There are a few different factors that caused you to go into panic, not just one."

Ana was so desperate to know the cause for her panic and what she could do to stop it. But unfortunately, there were no definitive answers, and the intense sensations just wouldn't relent.

She couldn't believe how endless it seemed. Every day, she thought it might end, and every day, it wouldn't. At one point, she even called a mental health hotline on the back of her insurance card, looking for answers. The person who picked up was very kind and soothing, but clearly a beginner, because they had to look up how long panic attacks lasted.

It should be around twenty minutes at the most, they told Ana. But unfortunately it was a lot longer than that because she was caught in a perfect storm.

Ana was no longer whole; her sense of self and her sense of time were warped.

There were moments when she would feel disconnected from herself, depersonalized. She would look at her hands and not recognize them as part of her own body. She avoided looking at herself in the mirror, as if she was tripping on acid, which she hadn't taken since high school.

Most of the ordinary facets of life were hard to manage. The caregiving and the householding. Walking the dog. The lights in the grocery store were too much, the sun was too bright. She couldn't handle being on screens for too long. Ana had to lean on Drew a lot more for the cooking and the cleaning.

She would push herself to go to mellow yoga classes, often just to have somewhere to go, to be around other people.

Sometimes she would find someone to talk to about her anxiety outside of her team of healthcare practitioners. Often it would be a yoga teacher or another student—she realized that most people didn't know how to talk about anxiety, or didn't want to.

A few days before the literary event, a writer friend texted to say that she would be coming to hear Ana read. Ana wrote this friend back right away and asked if she would read for her, how she wasn't feeling great, how she still had such a bad cough, something she picked up on the plane home from New York.

Her friend agreed to read for Ana. This calmed her down a bit; although she also felt guilty, shameful that she couldn't do it.

There was this push and pull inside of her, the tension of wanting to do it but also not being able to.

Ana's doctor prescribed her a handful of Xanax, to help pull her out of this nervous system takeover. It is a class of medicine that is known to be highly addictive, so it was meant solely for this urgent, triaging purpose. She didn't like how it made her feel, but it would give her a temporary break. The medicine would work for a few hours, and then Ana would just feel terrible again.

Another writer she knew, in town from New Mexico for the reading, stopped over with his girlfriend. Ana was still sick. Her cold had turned into this terrible cough that ended up lasting weeks. She didn't want them to get sick, so they sat on the front lawn, and Ana remembers feeling somewhat centered for the first time in days.

It was sunny, warm, pleasant and it felt like the ice in her bones was maybe starting to melt away. Ana knew that the writer-friend had been sober for a long time, and she became paranoid that they could tell she was altered from half a Xanax.

But the event later that evening was lovely.

A band played instrumental music and her friend read from Ana's story. In the end, sitting back and hearing her work read aloud was a profound experience—it felt as if something really came together.

All the years of the challenging work of unpacking and excavating the hard things through the writing—all that tension seemed to dissolve. She was able to bear witness and not be caught in it.

Ana wishes she could say that this was the end of the panic, but it was more like the beginning.

During this time, books became a refuge.

She recalls reading one about women abstract painters who lived and worked in the shadows of the more famous male painters of their time. Something about their cold water studios, how they often struggled to get by and their decisions to make art and not to raise children were intriguing and strangely comforting to Ana.

She brought the book with her to a cafe and the server was also reading it, so they chatted briefly. Ana cozied up in a nook to sip tea and to read, but just then a wave of panic came over her and she had to step outside.

Ana found a shady spot in a narrow alley. She called Drew. He picked up and acted ambivalent with her on the phone. Someone must have been with him in his studio, most likely his work partner, but he didn't say that.

> "Hey hon, sorry, I'm having a really hard time," Ana said, "I'm on Mississippi..."
> "Okay," he said, pausing.
> "Sounds like you can't talk, so I'll let you go," she said, tearing up.
> "Okay," he said.

This is the part of Drew that has always been hardest for Ana to accept. Ana wondered why he couldn't just excuse himself and step outside and talk to her. That's what she would have done. She hardly ever called him during the day.

> "He's kind of narcissistic," Jayne said to Ana one day.
> "You think so?" Ana asked, surprised.
> "Yes, I do," Jayne answered.

Ana knows that people tend to throw the word narcissism around willy-nilly. But she also knows that identifying when someone tends to operate from a narcissistic lens can be helpful. It's a coping mechanism, Ana has since come to understand. It is something you might learn as a child when your parents aren't responsive to your needs. But then you become an adult and the lens is still in operation unless you decide to replace it.

Ana took some deep breaths and went back into the cafe, where she was able to pour herself back into the book. It was reading about the artist's struggle that brought the most relief for Ana during those hardest of days. It helped her feel not so alone, offered a way of relating to her own pain.

There is a clean arc to this narrative, an exact point where the panic peaked.

A friend of Ana's was dying.

Well, they hadn't been friends in a few years. Ana had been avoiding this friend because she could be high-maintenance and self-centered.

They would meet for tea, and this woman would talk about her dysfunctional family relationships for a few hours, and then Ana would leave feeling depleted. She got nothing back from their friendship.

Ana stopped responding to her texts and phone calls, which set them up for awkward run-ins around town. When Ana would go to stores she knew the friend frequented, she would look to see if her car was in the parking lot. One time, Ana saw the woman in the produce aisle and turned around and quickly left the store.

And then a few years after she distanced herself, she heard that this former friend had late stage colon cancer. The woman was no longer in Ana's life, so even though she thought about visiting with her, maybe reconnecting at the end of her life, she decided against it.

It felt like too much considering the state that Ana was in. Ana had been starting to feel a little better by this point, so she was protecting herself.

Then right around the time that she heard that this ex-friend had died, there was a night when the panic and the despair hit its crest.

It was her dark night of the soul.

Ana couldn't sleep; she was awake until sunrise.

This had never happened to her before. Since the onset of the anxiety symptoms, she had only been able to sleep for maybe half the night, but was never unable to sleep at all.

On this particular night, Ana was up all night praying for relief, feeling her heart pounding away in her chest. She tossed and turned, just couldn't settle down.

At one point, staring at the wall in the attic, she thought about her grandmother, her mother's mother, and she remembered a song in Italian that she would sing to Ana as a child and that memory comforted her.

By morning, Ana was shaking uncontrollably, her heart continuing to race. She was out of her mind and body with panic and exhaustion. Somehow, she managed to get Lucien off to school and then she had Drew take her to urgent care. She knew that something wasn't right and she feared something was medically wrong with her.

The nurse at urgent care was a gray-haired, stocky man, so kind and concerned. He told Ana that he also struggled with anxiety. He put those sticky things on her chest and checked her heart, as she explained that it wouldn't stop racing. That's what happens when you are dropped so hard into panic. You think your heart is about to explode.

There was nothing wrong with her physically, other than a racing heart rate. Ana left urgent care that day with the knowledge that she wasn't dying and some more pills to help her sleep.

It took about six months and a lot of resources, medication, and support for Ana to even begin to feel better again.

When she has moments of clarity, the adult part of her can see that time as a way for her to wake up from many years of hiding from her past. The hyper-personal story about a hardscrabble childhood comes out and the writer comes completely apart.

And then Ana got sober.

It was something that she had been considering for years. She would take intermittent breaks but then she would turn back to the wine again. She knew for a long time, since her twenties really, that she leaned too heavily on weed and alcohol to feel calm. She hadn't been smoking pot as much in recent times, as it tended to make her paranoid.

There were several years when weed was her drug of choice, but then she had a full-blown freak out on pot in her friend's borrowed Paris flat and hardly ever smoked again after that.

It's a little funny to think about now, but she thought that the centuries-old, three-story building was about to collapse on top of her. It was evening and the light in the simple, yet beautiful flat had turned to a gentle dim. Lucien, who was five at the time, was asleep in the bedroom. Ana couldn't look at him. Watching him breathe was too much in her altered state.

She huddled by Drew's feet at the dining table like a frightened toddler, practically pulling at his pantleg.

"You're gonna be fine, hon," he said to Ana, smiling.
"But I'm freaking out!" she said.
"It's okay," Drew said, laughing.

They had brought two types of pot back from Amsterdam, one was the chronic insanity that Drew liked to smoke and then there was the super chill kind for Ana. The two types of weed must have mingled in the smoking device.

And then, about an hour into the ordeal, her mood made a complete turn for the absolute better.

Ana put on some ambient music and got into the bathtub. She wept, staring out the window onto the beautiful, tiled Parisian rooftops. The music mixed with the frenetic sounds of cars and motorbikes and bicycle bells, she couldn't remember a time when she was happier, more present—feeling the summer breeze, smelling the foods being cooked, hearing the clanking of the neighbors' dishes, the conversations in French.

She also couldn't enjoy pot again after that experience. Even though the part where she was blissed out in the tub was amazing, the part where she was paranoid was just too terrifying.

And the wine—the wine remained in her life for a good while longer.

And then it was gone forever.

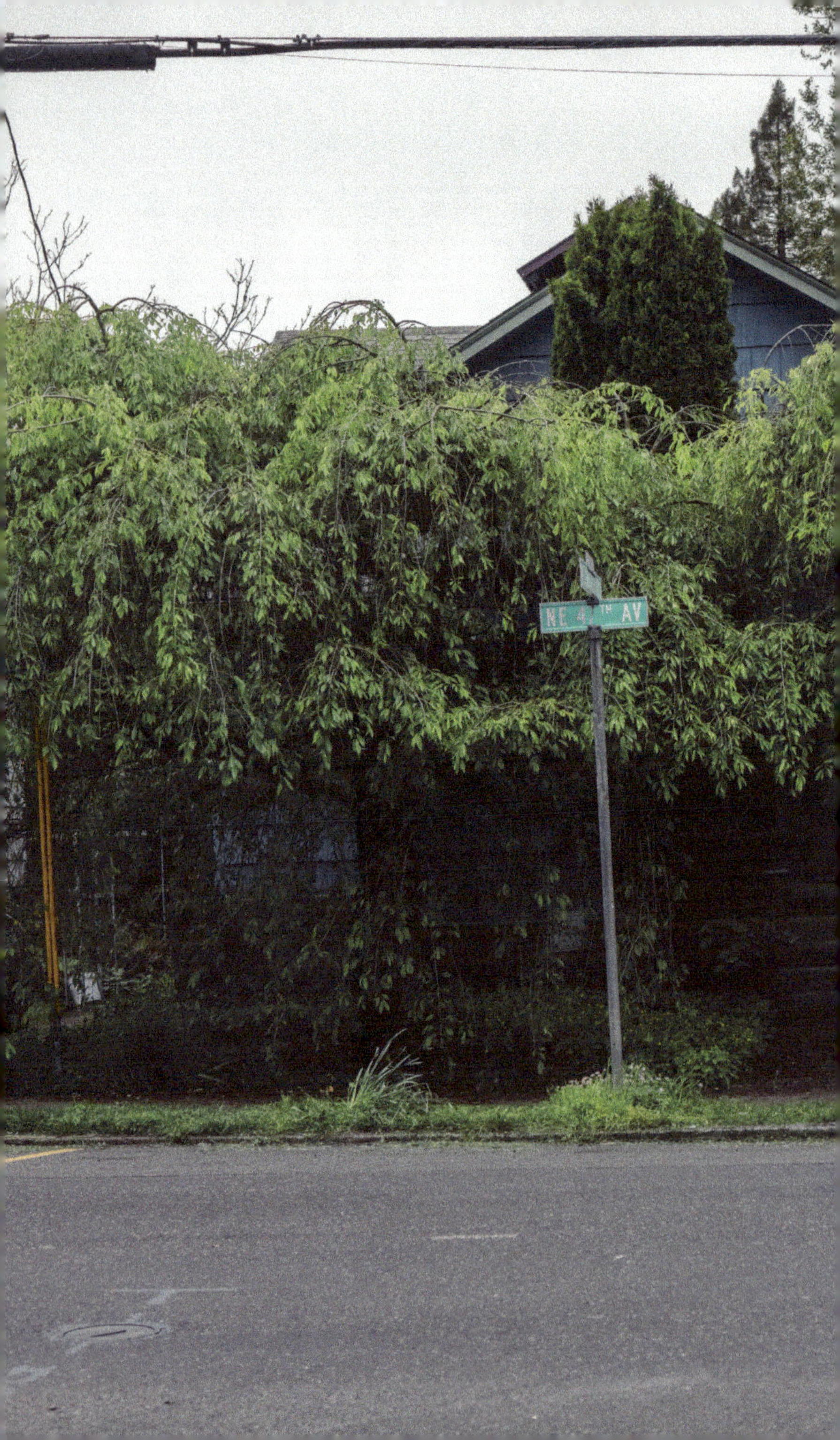
NE 47TH AV

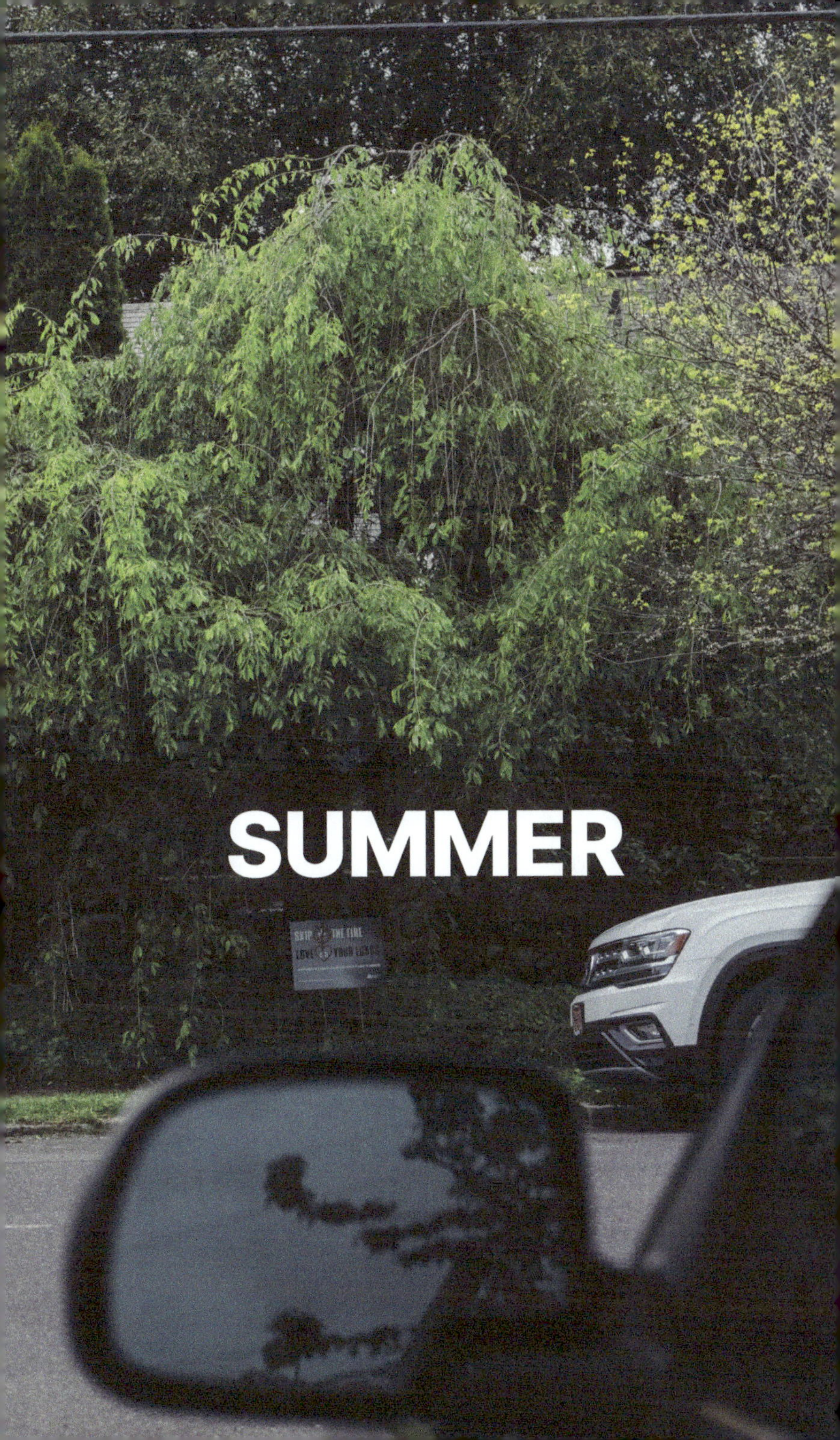

SUMMER
SKIP THE FINE
LOVE YOUR LOCAL

Ana returns from a writing retreat on the Washington coastline.

It was the first time she had been away from Drew and Lucien since her debilitating anxiety started. Leaving the nest had felt too vulnerable.

While she was away at the coast, writing and sipping tea and staring at a sunspot on the weathered wooden floorboards in solitude, everything that felt so fucked up about ordinary life faded away.

She felt safe and secure, more so than she had in a long time, as if she could handle anything that might come her way. Ana was able to see how important it is to work to heal our past wounds.

It's a ramshackle, vintage-style resort set in a sleepy seaside town. A Portland hipster bought it in recent years and made it into something of an artist's colony. She had been here a handful of times before, mainly to work on her writing, so there was a familiarity even though some time had passed.

Ana recalls one of her first writing residencies here, back when she was toiling away on some personal essays—it had to be almost ten years ago. Each day, all day, Ana would sit at a large round wooden table in the main lodge, getting up occasionally to flip a record or to refill her coffee. It rained a lot and she stood at the gas fireplace to warm up.

At the end of the day, she would take a sauna and chat to whoever else was around. There was a sense of belonging and community.

She has always found writing to be a challenging and often emotionally exhausting endeavor, so being around other people, but also tucked away in solitude is a perfect combination.

Ana took her favorite room in the lodge—the one with the amazing natural light. But things were altered this time. There was no communal gathering in shared spaces. The main lodge room was shut to guests and the sauna had to be booked ahead and taken alone.

Ana hardly spoke to anyone, but she relished the solitude. She had forgotten how nourishing it was to wake up and not have to feed the pets, to clean up the kitchen after a teen who eats cereal and ramen and peanut butter and jelly sandwiches after hours, to not be constantly turning over during the night to avoid a snoring spouse.

Ana had gotten lost when the anxiety hit, especially since it came on so hard and fast. Now, she was getting to know herself again after losing track the past few years. And creatively, there was an openness she hadn't been able to experience in a long time.

She can vaguely recall a movie in which someone's brother wanders off into the desert and doesn't remember who he is, or was. Ana related to that. She had to rebuild herself from scratch, cell by cell.

"You looked ragged," a friend said to Ana after the anxiety had waned.
"I did?" she asked in disbelief.

Ana knew what her friend meant but she couldn't believe that he was talking about her. It was always other people who looked ragged.

There are still times when she feels like she could easily fall off that edge again. But she has mostly learned how to nudge herself out of the eddy and push herself back onto land.

"It's always been there—you just weren't aware of it," Jayne said to her one day.
"Like it was hiding?" Ana asked.
"You couldn't allow yourself to feel it, you weren't ready," Jayne had said.

Ana couldn't comprehend it at the time because she was too strung out on bad sleep and jagged nerves. But she gets it now. You have a shitty childhood where you are exposed to all these micro traumas while your nervous system is under development. And then over time, you stockpile that constant stream of fear and anxiety. It lives deep in your body, and you tamp it down with wine and weed and gnarly yoga for years just to feel somewhat okay, until one day, something cracks you open and then you break the fuck apart.

Ana needed to break open because otherwise, she would probably never have been able to heal.

When Ana arrives home from her week at the coast, she spends a little time catching up with Drew and Lucien. What they ate. How often they walked the dog. Where the cat slept. She unpacks her things and notices that the fridge is looking sparse, so she bikes up to Alberta Street to grab a smoothie and some groceries.

It's mid-afternoon and the summer sun is blazing. She already misses the cool, coastal weather. Transitioning back to family life feels jarring. It's always like this for Ana, integrating back into the householder role after being away.

She does recall it being a lot more challenging when Lucien was younger, when he had more needs. It still feels like exhaustion, depletion, like you want to go back out the door and never return. It's kind of like when you have a friend who takes from you and doesn't give back. You just sit there listening to them talk at you and you constantly have to tend to their needs, but they never tend to yours. It kind of feels like that sometimes because parenting is pretty one-sided, as it should be, but the difference is that you are nurturing a human not feeding a narcissist.

So you get home and you acclimate. The overwhelm is fleeting and you settle back into the caretaking, settle back into the caregiving.

She leans her bike against a wall nearby, orders a smoothie, and asks the frazzled server how she's doing.

"Not great!" she shouts over the loud blending.
"I hear you!" Ana shouts back.

Ana leans on a wooden counter in the shade, reflecting on the week: working on her writing, having a daily sauna, meditating, taking long walks. Not worrying about food shopping and meals and cleaning up. Not having to caretake anyone but herself.

A young couple with a sleeping toddler sidles up to the cart and then another couple in athletic wear gets in line behind them. A couple with a baby and a few friends gather at a nearby picnic table, eating salads and drinking juices. Ana focuses in on the couple with the toddler, remembering when Lucien was that age, remembering how hard it was.

The kid was asleep when they got to the smoothie cart, but now he's awake and cranky so the mom picks him up and rubs his back. They give the child small sips of their smoothie. Ana can tell that they are tired. She knows the feeling.

Ana thinks about the smoothie-maker person saying she's not doing well, and decides not to ask why. We all know why we're not doing great. It has come to a point where we don't even need to ask each other anymore. It used to be we would always say we're doing good, now we always say we're hanging in there.

Ana needs to go to the co-op to get something simple to make for dinner. She finishes her smoothie and puts the jar on the counter.

"We're gonna be okay," Ana says to the smoothie-maker person.
"You sure?" she asks.
"Yeah, I promise," Ana says.

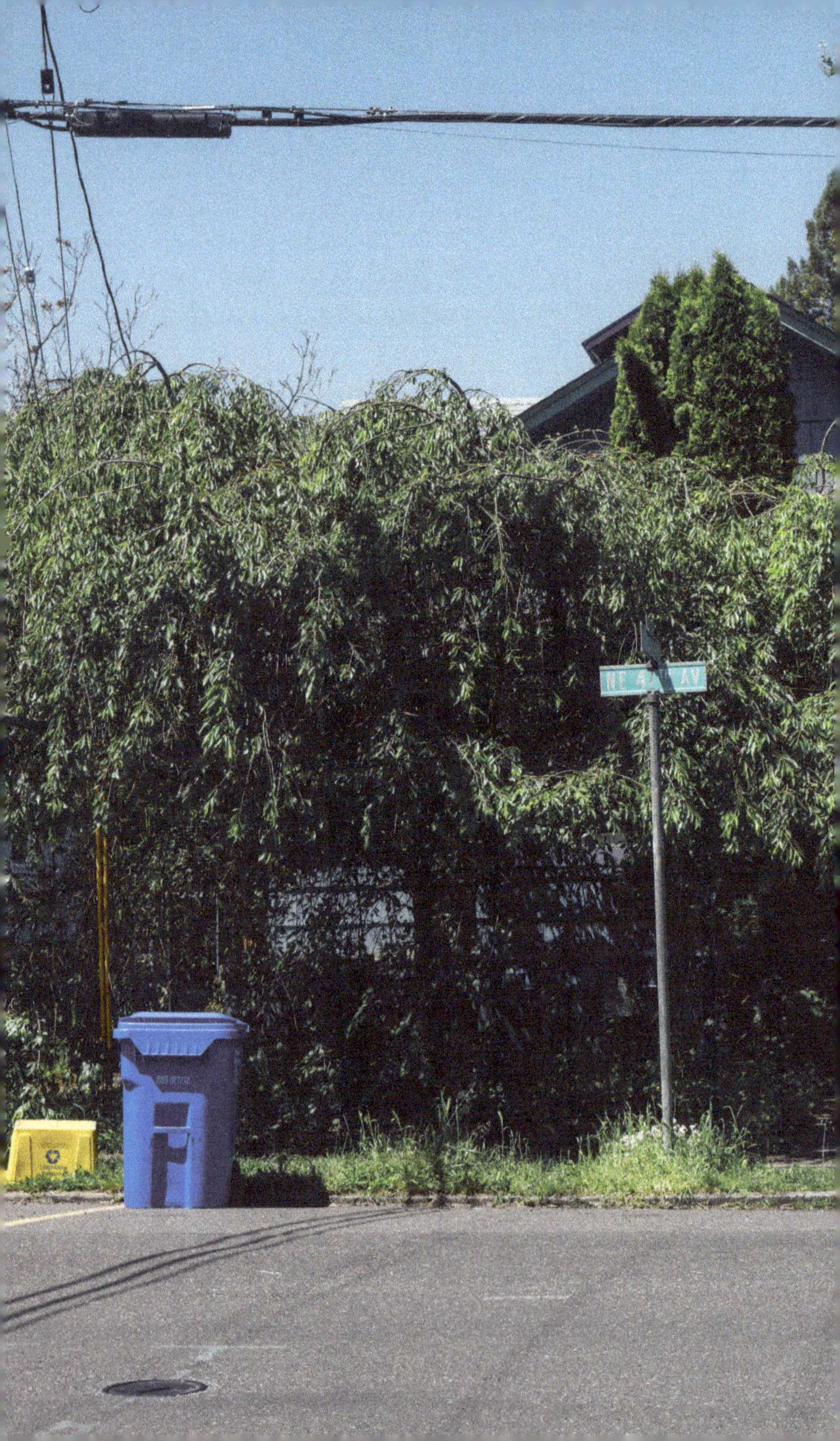

NE   AV

Ana asks Drew to quit smoking pot.

She's sitting at the kitchen table and he's standing near the sink. She just blurts it out and the next thing she knows, she's tossing a handful of buds and a couple of dried psychedelic mushrooms into their compost bin outside. And then she's upstairs in a closet looking for somewhere to stash his vape pen.

Ana opts for an empty file folder box, taking into consideration that Lucien is at the age where he and his friends are looking to get high. She is on alert these days because there was one time that they sort of caught Lucien with weed.

It was New Year's Day and he had recently turned thirteen. They had been to a friend's house the night before, bundled up in layers and huddled around a fire pit, trying their best to be festive and joyful. It was a raw, anxious time. The kids had been in online school since the previous spring and the isolation and extended screen time had been hard on the kids, hard on the parents.

Ana and Drew later found out that Lucien and a friend had colluded and met at a park armed with a loaded vape pen.

Ana had a feeling that Lucien was up to something because she had caught him rummaging around Drew's desk. It was late morning, and she was meditating in the attic. He must not have realized that Ana was up there, because she was tucked away in a quiet little nook.

"What are you looking for?" Ana called over.
"Just a Sharpie," Lucien said, clearly startled.

Ana's instincts told her that something was up, but she decided to let it go out of parental laziness. She had been monitoring the child's online schoolwork for months and midwifing him through preteen angst and anxiety. She was experiencing major caregiving fatigue.

When Lucien came home from the park a few hours later, Ana and Drew were drinking coffee with friends on the front porch, celebrating a new year, trying to feel hopeful in an unhopeful time. Lucien seemed extra chipper and chatty, laughing about randomly finding an apple in the street. That was when Ana knew that something was awry.

But she let it go, figuring she might bring it up later.

Ana was sitting at the kitchen table eating breakfast when she got a call from her good friend, the mother of the other kid Lucien was at the park with the day before. They mainly texted and hardly ever spoke on the phone, so she knew the call was urgent. Ana felt her heart pounding in her chest.

"The boys got into something," she told Ana right away.
"Okay," Ana said.
"They went to the park with a vape pen to try pot."

As her friend unraveled the story to Ana, she remembered catching Lucien rifling around Drew's desk and became frustrated with herself for not addressing it in the moment. She told Ana that her son confessed to his cousin who said if he didn't tell his parents, that she would, so he came clean.

Lucien had secured the vape pen and then the two boys convened at the park and took a few hits.

It was mid-morning and Drew was in bed, looking at his phone. Lucien was still asleep across the hall. Ana sidled up to Drew on the bed and told him what transpired.

It took him a few moments to come into the present.

"Really?" Drew asked.

"Yep," Ana said.

Drew put on some clothes, and they went upstairs to see if the vape pen had been returned. He looked around his desk and then started laughing. His legit vape was still in its hiding spot. It was another one that was missing.

"Dumb ass kids took your old CBD vape!" he said.

"Shut up! They did?"

"And it doesn't even fucking work...the battery is dead," he said.

Ana texted her friend right away to let her know that it was a botched attempt. Lucien must have thought that he got high, a placebo effect of sorts. But there was no way—there was hardly any juice left, the battery was dead or pretty much dead, and CBD might relax them, but it wouldn't get them high.

Ana and her friend were both relieved, but they also knew that it would be up to them to talk to the kids. The dads wouldn't do it or would do it in a shitty way so it would all be on them, the moms. But she knows that it would be worse to not talk to Lucien.

Her fear is that he could become derelict, wayward, kind of how Ana was at his age.

Ana's parents never spoke to her about sex, alcohol or drugs. They also didn't know what the fuck she did, when she did it, or who she did it with. She got caught getting drunk on Jack Daniels with two boys from her apartment complex when she was fourteen. Ana doesn't think her mother said anything to her about it. Her father took her on a car ride and bought her a milkshake as if she was a young child, but he didn't talk to her about what had happened.

Ana didn't feel seen or supported so she made terrible choices. She pushed the edge with drinking and messing around with boys.

Even though she knows that Lucien has so much more support and care than Ana or Drew ever got as kids—she still knows that he's a teenager with a developing frontal cortex.

When confronted about the vape pen incident—the child went under the duvet and wept. Ana sat with him for what felt like an eternity, hugged him when he would let her and cautiously nudged him to talk.

Drew stood by like an assistant. He's a terrible disciplinarian. The opposite of Ana, he was punished a lot as a child, shamed.

He prefers to avoid it altogether.

At first, Drew pushed back on quitting weed.

He stood by the kitchen sink with a rag in his hand, while Ana was across the room at the kitchen table, doing her best to stay firm.

"This is what addiction looks like," she told him.
"I enjoy smoking weed, hon!" he responded.
"I know you do, and I get it, but it's starting to effect you in different—"
"But I'm the same person that I always was," Drew said.

They had been through this before, Ana asking Drew to stop smoking weed. He'd stop for a few weeks, maybe a month until one day, he'd come home from his studio stoned and annoying the shit out of her.

When you used to smoke pot and are around a frequently stoned person, you know that they think everything is epic, when it's not really that epic at all. You're like, *yeah, okay, that band sounds cool and all, but it's not that cool.*

Ana thinks of a previous time when she begged Drew to quit smoking pot. They were at the coast. Lucien must have been back at the house because Ana and Drew were sitting on the beach and she was crying out of desperation, telling him that she needed him to be more present.

> "I need to feel like I could depend on you, like if something happens..." Ana said, sobbing.
> "I'm not gonna quit smoking pot, hon," he said. "I've been smoking since I was fifteen."
> "But I really need you to!" she begged.

He wouldn't relent, as if the weed was more important than she was.

She wanted Drew to do anything he could to help her feel better, because she felt so terrible.

They walked back to the cabin to check on Lucien.

Drew immediately grabbed his surfboard and left for a few hours. Ana recalls sitting on the deck in the sun, trying to release some of the difficult feelings—the fear and the frustration. She remembers putting her head in her hands and exhaling hard.

The reason she remembers is because, at this exact moment, their next-door neighbor walked by and asked if she was okay. He was concerned. Until then, nobody outside of her family unit or healthcare practitioners had witnessed Ana's crisis state.

She remembers trying her best to hold it together around Lucien. She could tell he knew she was struggling, but she made the decision not to broach it with him. Ana didn't think that the boy would be able to understand, that he was too young.

After she got better, she would think about bringing it up to him, but she has chosen not to. Not yet at least.

Drew agreed not to get high when she was around, which soothed her for a while. But one evening, not long after, he came home from his studio still high. As she had before, she chose to let it go, avoid, pretend that she didn't notice he was stoned.

That pattern would go on for months, the frustration building.

Ana and Drew used to get high together all the time. They would sit at the kitchen table with a bottle of red wine, chatting, sipping, and smoking. That is how they would relate to each other, and it worked for a while until it didn't because Ana decided to not lean on substances anymore.

Ana knows enough about substance use and abuse to know that the person must want to stop doing the thing. They must find it on their own, otherwise they'll circle back over and over and over again like Drew has through the years.

"How's it going with not smoking weed?" Ana asked Drew one morning.
"I smoked a few times…I still smoke at the studio," he said.
"You what?"
"Yeah, I have a stash there."

She didn't get angry with him. She just listened and encouraged him to not smoke at the office, that quitting means quitting. Ana had shared her feelings about Drew's pot use and the rest was on him.

"We need to think about us, about our family," she said to Drew.

"I do think about our family," he said.

"But getting high takes you out of the present and so you're not really here with us."

"I'm always here."

"Yeah, but it doesn't feel like you're here," Ana said.

There is a vacancy behind his eyes. She speaks to him, but she doesn't feel a connection or like her words are landing. Ana doesn't think he understands what it means to be present and what it means to truly connect with another person.

She will take anything other than the stoner bullshit at this point in her life. It's fun when you're in your twenties, but they are much older than that now and it's not a good look to be high and talking about dumb ass shit you see on the internet.

Ana realizes that Drew's pot avoidance is reminiscent of her parents' neglect. How when he's high and distant, she feels unsafe and ignored even while surrounded by family—this is how she often felt as a child. She is learning to see when her old conditioning gets triggered by present stimuli.

Ana's anxiety has begun to shift.

It used to be that she was always frightened, but her fears were about nothing specific. For most of the day and sometimes through the night, she would feel shaky inside and out, unsettled, scared. Sometimes she would worry about a natural disaster or something bad happening to Drew or Lucien or the animals, but most of the time, it was an impossible, generalized fear.

Once, coming home from a walk, all she could do was crawl into bed, burrow herself in the blankets, and scream at the top of her lungs.

Ana screamed for the fear to stop. *Stop it. Stop it. Stop it.*

Nothing would stop it, though. Not the warm baths or the long walks or the meditation or the yoga or the phone calls.

But then in time, the anxiety morphed into another form. It got more and more laser-focused. Eventually, it evolved into a deeply intense fear that something was physically wrong with her.

One day it could be a small lump on an arm, the next day, a miniscule red dot on her face.

Ana worries that she will find something, that she will have to get it looked at, tested, and wait weeks to find out that it's cancerous. She worries about having a stroke or a heart attack, being told she has a degenerative disease. She panics when she is due for routine bloodwork or a mammogram. She worries about getting results that would prompt the doctor to send her for follow up tests.

She must have developed this fear of illness after her mother was diagnosed with lung cancer and died within a year of her diagnosis.

When you see someone go through terminal lung cancer, the struggling to breathe because their lungs are filled with fluid, the nausea and vomiting from chemotherapy, the burning from radiation, the emergency room visits, the months of hospice, the weeks of morphine, it sinks into you.

The whole process is terrifying. And Ana was pregnant while her mother was dying.

She believes that as a protective layer—to stay sane while carrying a child during this cancer care—that she blocked out a lot of the scary parts of this time in her life. They got stashed for later.

"You will be fine no matter what happens to you, and you need to keep telling yourself that," Jayne told her.

Ana tries to comfort her younger self which feels awkward because she is her and they are not two people. She doesn't know how else to soothe her without making them into two separate people. Ana puts her hand on her heart and takes a few deep breaths.

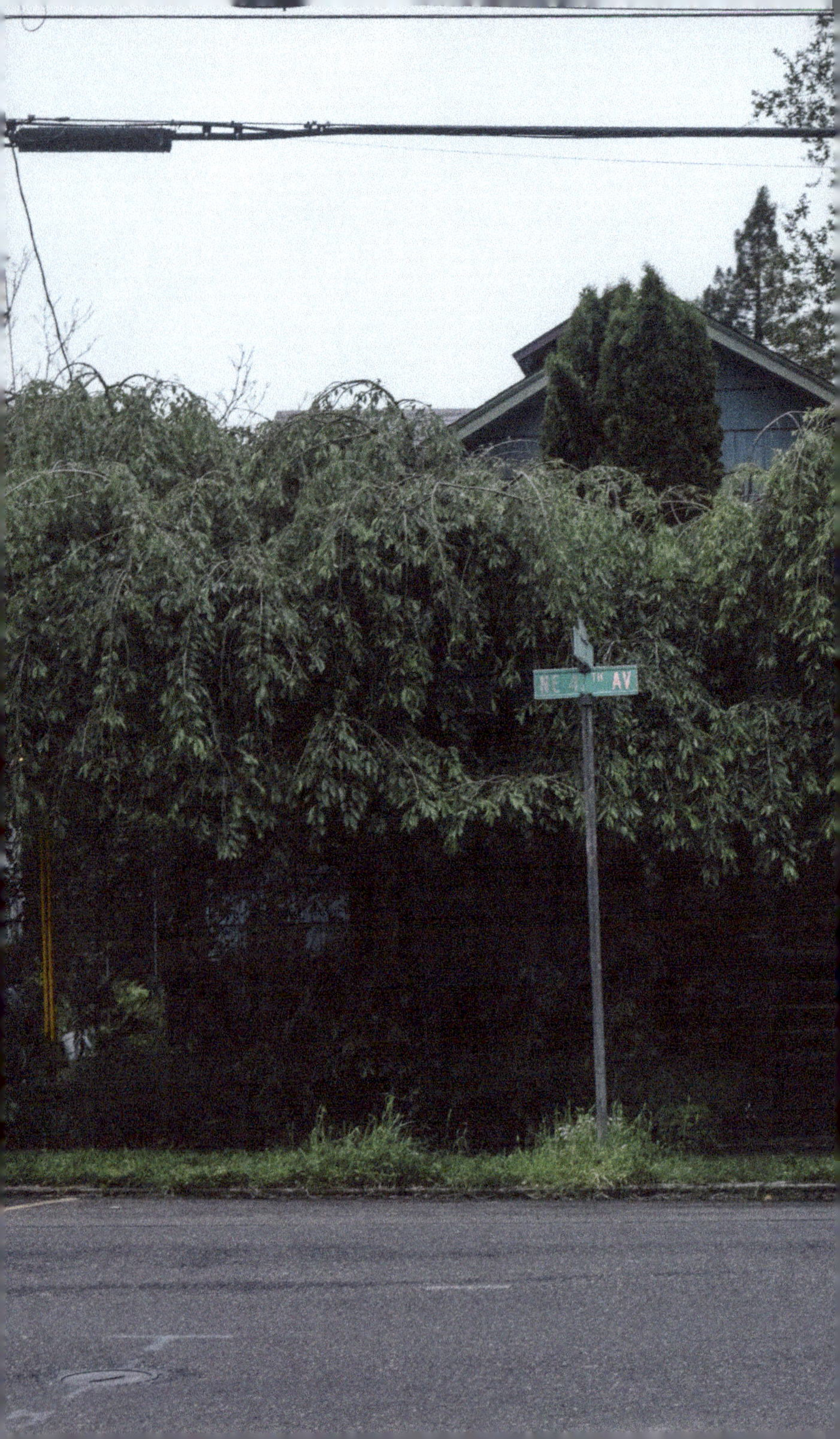
NE 4TH AV

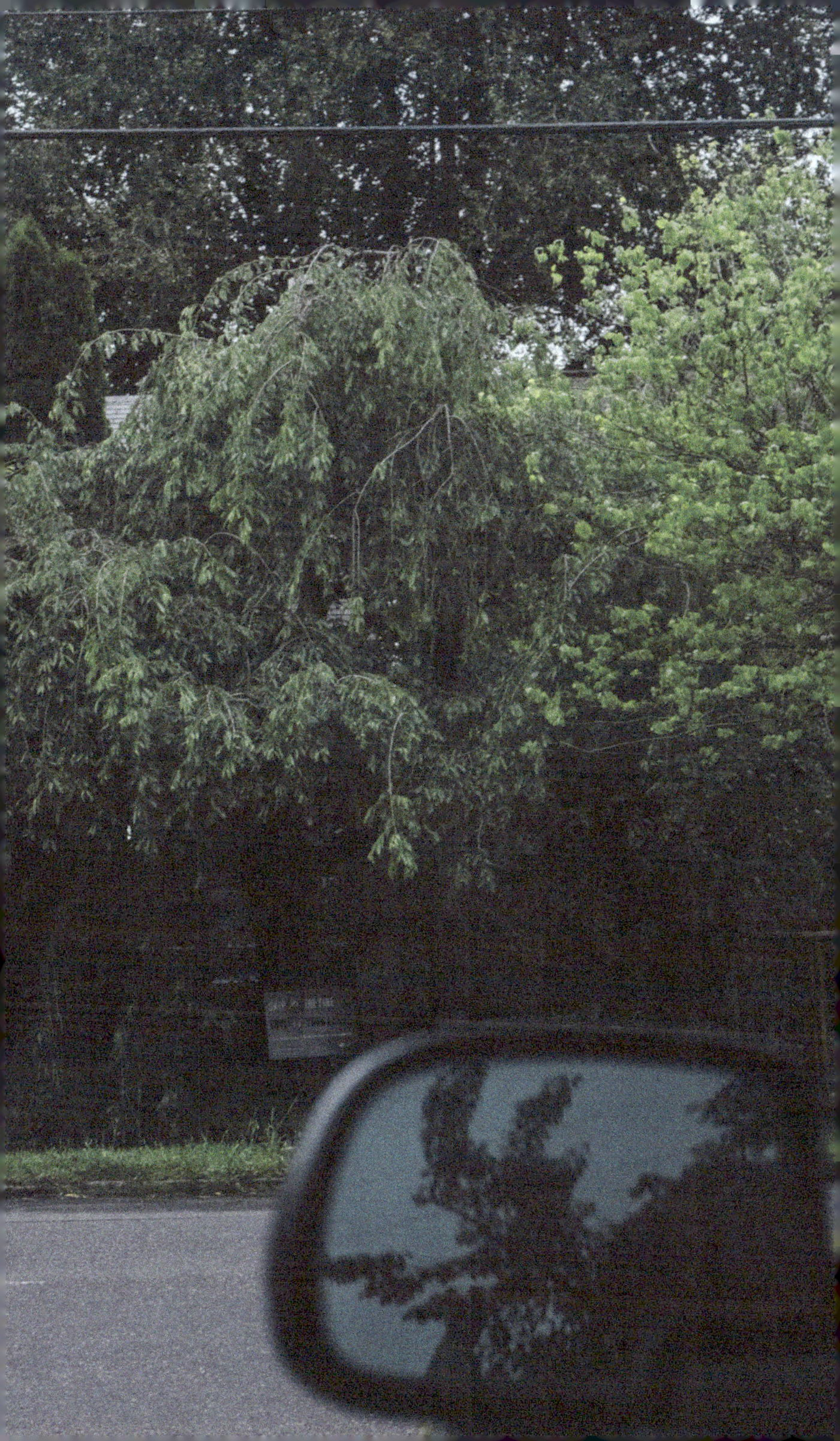

Ana makes her first trip to New York since her personal coming apart, and since the global coming apart.

They rent a studio apartment in the basement of a narrow row-house in the West Village that was built in the 1860s. There's nothing much to it–it has a queen-sized bed, a small pullout couch for Lucien and a basic kitchenette. It's on a relatively quiet side street in the middle of the busy hive of Manhattan.

Before settling in after a long day of travel, Ana walks down the block to a deli for breakfast supplies: Greek yogurt, too-sweet granola, some waxy apples, a few bananas, oat milk creamer and a small jar of honey for Ana's tea.

On her way back, she passes Leroy Street.

Like a flash, Ana recalls being completely obsessed with a barista who had a summer sublet on that block. It was decades ago, but she remembers it like it was two days ago. She was twenty, maybe twenty-one.

> Ana met him during one of her bartending shifts in Hoboken. They chatted and he told her where he worked, which was a coffee shop in SoHo. It was a time when coffee was just becoming trendy.
>
> He was tall and skinny with bright blue eyes and dark hair shaved into a buzz cut. He wore a pair of navy Dickies cut off just above the knees and a ratty white t-shirt. She had never been enchanted by anyone like she was with him before.
>
> It was a beautiful summer night and downtown Manhattan was bathed in glorious blue light when Ana and a friend stopped by his cafe, hoping he'd be working. They turned onto West

Broadway and there he was out front, taking a bag of trash to the curb.

He was surprised to see Ana. They were about to close, but Ana and her friend could still order coffees, he told them. They ordered cappuccinos and sat on a bench out front. Ana can recall the distinct coffee-infused smell of the bright cafe, she can hear the milk steaming.

He invited them out to a small club with one of his coworkers, so when they finished cleaning up and closing the coffee shop, they all walked there together. It was somewhere off Houston Street, not that far away.

Ana remembers feeling embarrassed by the clothing that her friend wore, like she was too Jersey. Ana was too Jersey too, but the friend was way more Jersey. They danced a little, and the barista sat on an old couch, drinking beer, and talking to his friends. A stranger told Ana that he liked how she danced.

The barista invited them back to his apartment, the one on Leroy Street.

Ana remembers that they all sat on the creaky hardwood floors, with their backs against the wall. There wasn't much furniture. She remembers that there was a clawfoot bathtub in the kitchen. His roommate was a liberal arts school graduate, the kind of person Ana felt envy towards in those days. She seemed smarter than Ana and was an earthy kind of pretty that comes with the comfort and ease of family money. The barista and his roommate clearly had a special kind of bond, as you do when you are in your early twenties and live together as close friends.

The two of them ended up spending the night together at her apartment back in Jersey with their hands all over each other, but the barista never called her back. That was back when you wrote your phone number on a scrap of paper. Waiting by the landline phone for days on end, she wondered if he lost the paper with her number on it.

Three years later, they ran into each other at a restaurant in SoHo where her good friend worked, and they hooked up again. He was a corporate coffee executive by that point, and Ana worked at an ad agency near Union Square. And again, it didn't amount to anything—he never called Ana back, but the way she felt about him, the severity of the crush, that lasted for many years.

"He's a Pisces," a friend of Ana said.
"What does that mean?" Ana asked.
"It means he's a floating cloud," she said.

Ana thought for sure that they would run into each other in another three years, but they never did.

Ana heads back to the apartment where Drew and Lucien are flipping channels on the television.

She unpacks the groceries and feels better now that they will have something to eat in the morning. She puts the fruit in a plastic salad bowl that she finds in a cabinet.

Ana takes a hot shower in the makeshift bathroom. Drying herself, she notices that the towels smell like urine. She doesn't think it's actually urine—she knows it's mildew. She goes on the Airbnb page, reads a comment that says the pillows smell like other people's heads.

Ana wakes in the middle of the night, forgetting she's not at home and feeling like her skin is crawling. She roots around in the dark for her herbs that calm the nervous system. Then she takes her pajama top and coils it around her face, so she doesn't smell the musty sheets and the pillows that smell like someone else's head.

Drew and Lucien don't mention the funky linens. They love the place. Ana decides not to mention anything, keeps it to herself and they spend the next week or so visiting with friends and family.

It's summertime hot and they walk many miles around the city, exhausted by the end of the day. Ana wakes up each morning before Drew and Lucien and walks the West Village. It has always been her favorite neighborhood in Manhattan.

When she passes Leroy Street, she looks down the block and searches her brain for which building the barista had his summer sublet in. But she can't remember.

One morning, Ana, Drew and Lucien get on Citi Bikes and ride across Manhattan to the East Village to get breakfast.

Lucien seems uncomfortable, unsettled. He only wants a fruit cup. Ana has a feeling that he's exhausted and that his stomach isn't right. She is also exhausted, and her stomach isn't right either.

She gets a message on her phone saying that she didn't put her Citi Bike back in the dock correctly, so Drew leaves the restaurant to go correct her mistake. She figures she does so much, that this is the least he can do for her. Ana planned the whole trip and has even procured coffee and chocolate croissants for Drew each morning.

They let Lucien walk around Manhattan alone for the first time. He wants to check out a few thrift shops and will walk back to the apartment by himself.

Ana is a little bit nervous, but also excited for him. She can't recall the first time that she walked the New York City streets alone as a kid. She would always go with a gaggle of friends, maybe a boyfriend, but never alone–not until she got her first job in Manhattan.

Lucien leaves the restaurant and they watch as he ventures onto the city streets.

Ana and Drew and make plans to go to an art exhibit in Chelsea. But after they pay the check and get back to the bikes, Ana decides that she wants to go to The Whitney Museum alone.

"I'll go to the MOMA then," Drew says.
"You sure?" Ana asks him.
"Yeah, that's fine, hon."

Ana feels a sense of relief and freedom, probably what Lucien felt walking off into the East Village by himself, away from his parents. She likes the idea of them all doing their own thing for a few hours.

Ana recalls a glorious, rainy afternoon spent alone at the Rijksmuseum in Amsterdam.

The friend she was staying with had a volatile

relationship with her ex and he would come into the flat in the mornings and yell. He had moved out months prior, but still had a key. It was awful waking up to that every day during the trip. Ana knew them well enough to know that this was their pattern, but that didn't make it any easier.

After a few days, Ana told her friend that she needed a day to herself.

It was pouring down rain and her shoes got wet, but she didn't care. Ana was so relieved to take a break from that cycle of abuse and to envelope herself in the Dutch Masters. Moving from canvas to canvas and escaping into the paintings felt as if she was floating through time.

She recalls sitting for a long while in the museum cafe with a latte and a slice of apple cake.

The sense of calm was palpable—she can still feel it now.

By the time she got back to the flat, her friend was stoned out of her mind on hash brownies, cleaning the house, probably trying to escape from her usual daily hell.

Now, there's no rain, the sun is heating up the streets and Ana looks forward to spending a few hours alone in a cool museum. The last time that she was in Manhattan, Ana had a wonderful afternoon alone at The Whitney and she longed to recreate that experience.

Ana used to tell people that her favorite thing in life was going to the movies alone, but now it's museums. When she goes with other people to a museum or a gallery, she can't enjoy the artwork as much. Ana can feel the emotions of the art in a way that would be interrupted if she was concerned with someone else's needs.

When Ana lived and worked in New York City in her twenties, she didn't have a partner or a family. She had a lot of freedom and a lot less stability.

She now realizes that she has traded in her freedom for stability, something that she didn't have as a child or young adult.

When Ana was done with college and working, she struggled to pay rent and bills, to eat well.

She didn't have stability, but she had freedom.

We get to choose, Ana thinks. We have to.

We get to decide between stability or freedom. And maybe we are lucky enough to have both. She's not there yet, she thinks. And though she's known both, for now, she chooses stability.

Ana spends a few hours alone with the art. She feels a deep well of emotion sitting with the abstract expressionists. She thinks about the book she read when she was riddled with anxiety, the one about women artists who gave up the stability of family life for freedom to make art during a time when most women didn't have that choice.

They made beautiful art, but it is full of struggle.

Ana sits on a bench near a large wall of windows in a spot of sun, overlooking Manhattan.

She looks at her phone and can see that Lucien is now back

at the Airbnb. He's probably tired. Ana has brought them to New York, to the city that she has always considered home. She made them sit through long dinners with family, with her good friends—she wants them to know this part of her, the part that was once free.

Lucien is older now and for the first time, he can see his mother in her former life.

> "I used to work up there," Ana tells Lucien, as they walk past a building where she worked in the Flatiron district.
> "Oh yeah?" he says.
> "I used to come here for cappuccinos when I was around your age," she tells him when they walk by an old cafe in the West Village that has never changed.
> "That's cool," he says.

He acts like he doesn't care, but she knows he does, or that someday he will at least. Because he might have to choose between freedom and stability.

Ana can feel the convergence.

Someday, maybe she will go back to her life of freedom, she thinks. Maybe when Lucien is out of the house, launched, secure in his own life, maybe even stable and free, she can rent something small in Manhattan or Brooklyn with a pullout couch for when Lucien visits.

She could go to museums alone. Maybe she will have more success as a writer. If she could support herself with that, she would be awarded freedom.

But Ana wouldn't leave Drew.

She plays back a fantasy, picturing them both on different sides of the country, he at their beach cabin surfing in the mornings and Ana here in the city, looking at art and working on her writing. A couple that lives between coastlines.

But for now, they return home to Portland. They return to the clean sheets and towels, to the organic food, to managing the budgets, to waking up each morning and tending to the pets and the home and the child.

Ana chooses her life again. For now.

POSTSCRIPT

I still write in the same cafe on Northeast Alberta Street that I worked in when I first started writing this book. The name of the cafe is different now, but I still call it by the old name.

Here I am, continuing to skirt around the writing, still fumbling with the music and checking the emails and text messages because it's hard to do the actual work.

The book is different, but it's also the same book.

When I didn't generate an income, my value came with the amount of effort that I put into the householding and the caregiving. And especially when Lucien was little, it never felt like I was off the clock.

Drew made the money and when it came to the house and the child, he took on the role of helper.

We both had challenging roles. Where Drew's role came with respect and admiration, my job description was mom who spends too much money on books and organic rice bowls.

That's how it felt, at least.

"You do what you want, when you want," Drew's brother said to me once.

Hearing that comment, I shut down. I didn't even have a response.

I understand now that I was seen as a kept woman.

I want to make excuses for all the privilege in this story.

I want to say that it's okay for me to have all these privileges because I had a fucked-up childhood.

I see you, Ana.

I see your anger and your resentment, but these emotions don't belong to you.

They belong to your mother.

If my boat had a hole in it, I don't know if Drew would save me. I know that he wants to be able to save me, it's just that he doesn't know how. He never learned.

But it's okay now because I have learned how to save myself.

This is that story.

Frances Badalamenti is the author of the novels, *I Don't Blame You* and *Salad Days*. Her essays and interviews can be found in *The New Yorker, The Believer Magazine, BOMB Magazine, Longreads* and elsewhere. She lives in Portland, Oregon, where she teaches workshops and mentors writers.

Aaron Wessling is a Portland-based photographer and co-founder of The Portland Darkroom. His recent work explores themes of impermanence and memory. His photography has been displayed at the International Center of Photography, Blue Sky Gallery, Newspace Center for Photography, and LightBox Photographic Gallery.